PRAISE FOR
THE HEART OF EVERYTHING

"The new Marc Levy tugs at our heartstrings from the first page to the last. We may all know that ghosts don't exist in real life, but we go along for the ride—and laugh, often with tears in our eyes. This is a joyful and tender novel about the father-son relationship."

—*Le Parisien*

"Light and funny, Marc Levy's newest is reminiscent of the Golden Age of Hollywood's greatest comedies. The reader will relish in its most hilarious moments. Beyond pure comedy, this novel has a personal touch, one that lies beneath the surface of many of Levy's books—that of his father's shadow."

—Agence France-Presse

"Funny and moving. It's the story of the love between a man and a woman, and a father and his son. It's about love and belonging—it takes us back to the fundamentals."

—Europe 1

"A book dedicated to parental and filial love."

—France Info

"A magnificent conversation between father and son. I loved it, and I'm not the only one!"

—*C à Vous*, France Télévisions

"This novel has the light elegance of some American comedies . . . Funny, lighthearted, yet thoughtful—it's pleasant to be haunted by this ghost in love."

—*La Voix du Nord*

"A daring, lighthearted and moving comedy about love and the father-son bond. Full of unexpected situations, and smart and stirring dialogue."

—RTL Radio

"It's lively, funny and serious all at the same time, as Marc Levy makes the reader think about their own relationships with their loved ones, about that unspoken love."

—Matthieu Marin, *Ouest-France*

"The author lets us share in a father/son relationship through dynamic, crazy, funny dialogue. This new book mixes emotion and humour effortlessly."

—*Le Progrès*

"A really endearing ghost story. Marc Levy summons the supernatural and builds a story you really want to believe in."

—*Elle*

"A funny, moving journey of discovery."

—Nikos Aliagas

"A poignant father-son road movie. It's the book to bring in summer."

—BFMTV

"This ghost story, so modern, is a real fairy tale for grown-ups. It's light, joyful, full of optimism."

—*Télé Z*

"This novel opens the door to those internal conversations that you never got to have with those who have passed on."

—*Midi Libre*

"An imaginative story, in the vein of his first novel, *If Only It Were True*. But more than anything, a good reason to talk about father-son relationships."

—*La Presse*

"Funny, tender, fantastic, the new Marc Levy novel is perfect for the holidays."

—*Télé-Loisirs*

"Marc Levy signs off on a tender and comforting twentieth novel."

—*Télé 7 Jours*

"Marc Levy's new novel warms the heart. *Ghost in Love* promises a triumphant adventure."

—*Lire*

The Heart of Everything

OTHER TITLES BY MARC LEVY

P.S. from Paris

All Those Things We Never Said

The Last of the Stanfields

The Strange Journey of Alice Pendelbury

A Woman Like Her

Hope

Just Like Heaven

The Heart of Everything

A Novel

Marc Levy

Translated by Maren Baudet-Lackner

Previously published as *Ghost in Love* by Versilio/Robert Laffont in France in 2019. Translated from French by Maren Baudet-Lackner. First published in English by Amazon Crossing in 2026.

Published by Amazon Crossing, Seattle
www.apub.com

EU product safety contact:
Amazon Media EU S. à r.l.
38, avenue John F. Kennedy, L-1855 Luxembourg
amazonpublishing-gpsr@amazon.com

ISBN-13: 9781662532795 (paperback)
ISBN-13: 9781662532788 (digital)

Cover illustration and design by Kimberly Glyder
Cover image: © Alexander Spatari, © Westend61 / Getty;
© Viorel Sima / Shutterstock

Printed in the United States of America

THE HEART OF EVERYTHING

PROLOGUE

You were eight years old. I was making breakfast while you gathered your things and put them into your backpack for school. Hearing your footsteps as you came into the kitchen, I turned around. You looked straight at me, your eyes wide, and asked, "Hey, Dad? What does it mean to be a father?"

After a moment's silence, I said, "How about some eggs?" I was unable to reply with the few simple words you expected. My answer to your question could be found elsewhere: in my smile, in the look in my eyes, in my needing to know what you were willing to eat—not just for breakfast that morning, but for the rest of the day and all the days that followed. Maybe those things *are* what it means to be a father, but I didn't know how to explain that to you. A kitchen table and forty years stood between us. As I looked at you, it occurred to me that I should have grown out of my selfish adolescence sooner, met your mother sooner, and conceived you sooner. Maybe you and I would have been closer if there'd been fewer years between us. I probably never answered you that day, but I never stopped asking your question of myself. Later, after I was gone, you started looking for your own answers, studying the precious moments we'd shared, replaying our past conversations. You began to unearth all those buried memories, carefully organizing them like you did your schoolbooks and notebooks in your backpack that morning. Trying to understand us better. Life is a strange game. Is that why I'm back here now? To bring us closer together now that you are not just my son, but also a man?

1

The Salle Pleyel concert hall was empty and dim. Beyond its walls, the spring sunlight was warming the city after a mild winter, but within them, only a single beam of light cut through the darkness to illuminate the stage, enveloping the piano in a halo of floating dust.

Rachmaninoff's Piano Concerto No. 2 is an intellectual piece. The kind that virtuosity alone cannot conquer. Each time Thomas played it, he found himself questioning every skill he thought he had mastered. Today, it also felt like he was searching for the invisible, experiencing at once all of the emotions he had ever felt, as if a path had been drawn from his first memories of childhood all the way to the next day, when a thousand people would come to listen to his performance and a few discerning ears would judge it. As he struck the final chord, the beam of light blinked three times. The lighting engineer was growing impatient.

"I know, I'm almost done. Just once more and I'll be out of here," Thomas called in the direction of where the man was working backstage.

"You've got it down, believe you me," a voice called back.

Others might have laughed off the musical advice of a lighting engineer, but Thomas trusted Marcel's ear. After all, the man had attended even more concerts than Thomas had. Marcel had operated the lights for orchestras from all over the world, so why should his opinion be any less valid than that of Thomas's conductor, who hadn't even deigned to attend his final run-through?

"I have to get home, Mr. Thomas, and I can't lock you in, though I'm sure you would love that. Go think about something else for a while. You must have something better to do at your age than spend the night here." Marcel approached the stage, his potbelly as prominent as his good nature. "I'm telling you, you've got this. Rachmaninoff is rejoicing as he watches you from heaven, believe you me."

"I'd rather he listen than watch." Thomas closed the cover over the keys. "And what makes you so sure he got into heaven? That monster composed some of the most difficult scores ever written."

"That's exactly how I know he's up there." The lighting engineer escorted Thomas to the stage door. "Fine, we'll agree he's listening. But let me just say, I watch you from my booth, and I see and hear the music coming from every part of you, even your eyes. Even when they're closed. If you play that way tomorrow, it'll be a triumph."

"You're too kind, Marcel."

"Don't be ridiculous. Kind! I'll show you kind! Get out of here." The technician pushed Thomas out the door. "My wife is waiting for me, and if I stay here any later, the reception she gives me will be anything *but* kind. Go spend time with your girlfriend or do whatever you want, but stop letting your nerves control you. No good ever comes of that. See you tomorrow. I'll be here an hour early if you want to practice one more time."

Pianists are overcome with loneliness the moment they walk out the stage door. Thomas sometimes envied flautists, violinists, and bassists, who all took their instruments with them when they left the hall. He stuffed his hands into the pockets of his blazer as he walked up Rue Daru, wondering what he should do with himself. He could call his longtime best friend and invite him to dinner at a brasserie, but Serge had just gone through a breakup, and the very thought of making conversation with him exhausted Thomas. Philippe would have been excellent company, but he was filming a commercial somewhere between

Poland and Hungary. François's gallery was nearby, within walking distance, but the week before, Thomas had chosen to practice rather than attend the opening of his friend's most recent show, and François knew how to hold a grudge. As for Sophie, she hadn't been answering Thomas's messages lately. She was probably putting an end to their on-again, off-again, mostly text-based relationship, no longer willing to welcome him into her bed whenever he sought a bit of warmth. Or maybe she'd met someone else. If so, it wouldn't last. Sooner or later, she'd be the one calling Thomas.

As he walked past La Lorraine brasserie, Thomas noticed a couple sitting together. Given how they were gazing at the Place des Ternes, they could only be tourists or new lovers. He crossed the street and headed toward the flower market at the center of the roundabout, where he picked out a heady bouquet of freesia and star jasmine. White flowers were his mother's favorite.

Bouquet in hand, he climbed aboard the 43 bus and took a seat by the window. Passersby hurried down the sidewalk. When the bus stopped at a red light, a strikingly graceful young woman pulled up beside it on her bike. She placed her hand on the window to avoid taking her feet off the pedals and smiled at Thomas. When the bus started forward again, Thomas looked back and watched her disappear into the traffic on Rue de Monceau.

In that moment, a memory rose to the surface of his mind. Thomas was twenty, with his father, the two of them on their way to the opening of a new exhibition by a Danish master. As they left the Jacquemart-André Museum, Thomas met the eyes of a woman coming toward them on Boulevard Haussmann. She passed them and continued on her way. Noticing their exchange of glances, Thomas's father took the chance to say he saw the street as an endless source of new acquaintances, a place where anything was possible. Too many idiots wasted their time trying to woo women in bars, or shouting out unintelligible conversations over the din of clubs and trendy restaurants. Raymond, though, was a natural Casanova—the complete opposite of his son, whose friends often teased him for his shyness.

Thomas got off at the Haussmann-Miromesnil stop and made his way toward Rue Treilhard. He pushed through the building's huge front door and, minutes later, rang the bell of a fifth-floor apartment.

"Don't you have your keys?" Jeanne asked, surprised, as she opened the door in her bathrobe.

"I gave them back to you—oh, I don't know, maybe ten years ago?"

"Such a sweet way to greet your mother. And those flowers, are they for me or do you have a date?"

"Is there anything good in the fridge?" Thomas slipped into the entryway.

"So, they're for me, then." Jeanne took the bouquet. "They smell strong," she added as she walked into the kitchen.

"A simple thank-you would have sufficed," said Thomas.

"Don't ever expect a woman to thank you for flowers. Instead, watch to see how carefully she arranges them in a vase. Didn't your father teach you that?"

Thomas opened the door to the refrigerator and then turned toward his mother. "Can I eat the ham?"

"You make such fascinating conversation, sweetheart! Good thing you'll be dining alone tonight. I'm going out and have no intention of changing my plans. But you're welcome to stay as long as you like. You can even sleep over if you want."

Thomas put the plate down on the table and hugged his mother tightly.

"Is something wrong?" he asked sweetly.

"You're squishing me," she said, amused, as she extricated herself. "The real question is, What's wrong with you?" Jeanne stood on her tiptoes to reach a vase on a top shelf. "Is it your concert that's got you in such a state? Don't worry, we'll do what we always do: I'll pretend I'm not coming, to avoid adding to your stress. As the doting mother of an ungrateful son who couldn't be bothered to reserve me a seat in the front row, I shall remain tucked away, out of sight in the back of the hall."

Feeling a mix of annoyance and affection, Thomas pulled two tickets out of his pocket. "One for you and one for Colette, but make sure she doesn't clap at the end of every movement. It's embarrassing."

"I'll do my best." She took the tickets and slipped them into the pocket of her robe. "You still haven't told me what I did to deserve such a beautiful bouquet," she said, putting the finishing touches on the arrangement. "The scent is a bit too strong for my bedroom. You don't mind, do you?"

"It's the fifth anniversary of Dad's death. I didn't know if you'd remember, but I wanted to be with you . . ."

"Oh, sweetheart. He may have left you five years ago, but he left me long before that. So, anniversaries, you know, they don't mean so much to me."

"You should go get ready," suggested Thomas. "I don't know what your 'plans' are, but it's getting late."

"If I bore you that much, feel free to eat in the kitchen," Jeanne said, and then she slipped away to her room.

Thomas watched as she walked down the hallway of the Haussmann-style apartment he'd grown up in. Then he attacked his plate of ham while checking his messages. Philippe had texted news from the set, some complaints about the snow and about how hard it was to manage a team that spoke barely a word of French and hardly more than that of English. He reported that Warsaw was beautiful, though, and Polish women even more so. Thomas had to agree. He'd been invited to play there by the city's Philharmonic Orchestra, and he remembered the concert fondly, the hotel he'd stayed in less so.

He loved going on tour. It was an unparalleled privilege to travel the world and play with musicians from all different backgrounds. But his career as a soloist had had an impact on his love life as well.

For a time, he'd had a passionate relationship with Anna, a Sicilian violinist he'd met on tour in Italy two years earlier. Over the span of six months, they'd managed to spend one December weekend together in Berlin, thanks to Shostakovich; a Thursday night in Milan in March, brought together by Bach; and a Friday in May in Stockholm, gripped in a Brahms-inspired fever. Brahms's Piano Concerto No. 1 in D Minor had accompanied their night together, and they'd decided it was their song. For a pianist and a violinist, making love to a Brahms concerto is an unforeseen source of wonder.

They went their separate ways in June, and July kept them apart. Grieg tried in vain to rekindle their flame in September, but not even Vienna could seal the deal. Their story came to an end in Madrid at the beginning of winter. Ever since, every time Thomas had played Brahms's Concerto No. 1, the conductor had had to instruct him to take his interpretation of the adagio down a notch.

"Are you staying?" his mother asked from the doorway.

Thomas stood and carried his plate to the sink.

"Leave it. I'll take care of it. I like doing the dishes after you've gone. It makes me feel like you still live here."

"I'm going to head home," he said. "I need to get a good night's sleep for tomorrow."

"Did you really put us in the eighth row?"

"They're the best seats in the house."

"Meaning, you're sure you won't see me sitting there, right?"

"You know why, Mom."

"Just once, one time in your whole life, you thought you read disapproval in my eyes while you were playing. You were sixteen and still at the conservatory. Don't you think it's time you let that go?"

"I didn't *think* I saw it, I *did* see it, and I blew my performance because of it."

"Maybe my eyes weren't lying then. Perhaps you had already messed up, from the very first notes. But you've more than made up for it in the years since, that's for sure."

"You know what they say: 'An adult is just a child with debt.'"

"And you'll be in my debt forever, sweetheart. In the meantime, you can stay as long as you like."

"Do you have any cigarettes lying around, by any chance?"

"I thought you quit."

"That's why I don't have any cigarettes."

"You'll find a pack in your father's desk. Colette smokes in secret during our Saturday-night dinners. It's rather pathetic at her age. She 'forgets' her pack, leaving it in the right-hand drawer, I think, or sometimes in the left-hand one, to spice up her next visit. What do you think of my outfit? Have I still got it?"

Thomas studied his mother's black pencil skirt and white top. Age seemed to have had little impact on her graceful figure and her natural elegance, and even less on her impulse to provoke.

"That depends on the age of your date," he answered innocently.

"How dare you!" she exclaimed, feigning outrage. "I'll get you back the next time you need my advice, you'll see. Fine, I'm leaving. I'm already late. Don't have too much fun without me!"

She hummed as she left—an obviously deliberate, and successful, attempt to annoy her son.

Thomas stepped into the office and rifled through both drawers of the desk before finding the pack he was looking for under a pad of paper. He opened it and was surprised to find, rather than cigarettes, six masterfully rolled joints.

Thomas had only smoked pot once in his life. Back when he was a preteen, his father had traumatized him with warnings about the devastating effects of drugs on young minds. Wielding photographs and recent studies, he'd presented irrefutable proof that the consumption of illegal substances could damage the nervous system and dash Thomas's hopes of becoming a concert pianist. Having a surgeon for a father was not without its drawbacks.

Since transgression is an integral part of life's lessons, however, Thomas had risked it anyway—just once, on a weekend trip to Normandy with his friends. Thomas had waited until the second night to commit his act of rebellion, to make sure those who had smoked the night before didn't present any neuromotor deficiencies. To be absolutely certain, he had made Serge and François complete a series of tests, including a three-legged race, a cup-and-ball game, and darts. As revenge, his friends made his first joint extra-strong. Thomas spent most of the evening with a goofy smile on his face as he admired what appeared to be a cow nestling between two of the ceiling beams in the manor they were staying in.

But tonight Thomas felt an irrepressible urge to smoke again, and since the joint he was holding belonged to Colette—his mother's best friend, who had just celebrated her seventieth birthday—he figured it couldn't be too dangerous. Besides, he'd only take one puff, two max. The end of the paper cone crackled as he moved the lighter's flame closer. The first puff filled his lungs, and since he'd never really quit smoking, he exhaled with a feeling of deep enjoyment. The second delivered the calming effect he needed, and the third would be the last, he swore. But then came the fourth. Thomas felt his head start to spin, and he stubbed out the joint in the ashtray. He staggered as he stood up to get some air.

As he grasped the handle to the French doors, which remained closed, he heard a voice behind him suggest it would be unwise to lean over the balcony in his current state. His blood instantly froze in his veins, because he recognized that voice.

It was his father's.

2

This was much more than a simple high. This was a feeling of vertigo, terrifying for a man who hated losing control of himself. The precision of Thomas's movements determined his future on a daily basis. This was the case for any pianist, just as it was for surgeons—surgeons like his father, whom he'd just heard speak from beyond the grave.

Thomas clung to the glass, fixing his eyes on the balcony of the apartment across the road, trying to keep his body from swaying.

"You can let go of the handle. No one has ever fallen through a closed door," the voice joked.

"You warned me about this," Thomas sputtered. "What have I done? What was in that joint? I've damaged my neurons permanently!"

"Calm down please, Thomas," scolded the voice. "You smoked a joint—not your first and surely not your last. I'll confess, my warnings were a bit over the top when you were a teenager. But I was afraid you'd try hard drugs. Anyway, the fact that you're hearing me tonight has nothing to do with that."

"'Nothing to do with that'?" repeated Thomas, his face still pressed against the glass. "I'm hearing the ghost of my father! Oh God, everything's spinning. I'm done for."

"Leave God out of it. And the 'ghost' talk, too, if you don't mind. You're having a panic attack, which isn't surprising given the circumstances. Do you remember the little trick I taught you to cope with your stress before going onstage? Place your hands over your mouth, then take deep breaths through the nose. The CO2 will do the trick, you'll feel better in no time. If I could hold you up, I happily would, but I don't have energy enough for that. It already takes a lot of work to be able to talk to you."

Thomas felt his legs give out as he slid down the glass of the door. Once he reached the wood floor, he curled into a ball and tucked his head between his knees.

"Come on, Thomas, stop acting like a child. It was just a joint."

"The first time I smoked, I saw flying cows, and now I'm hearing my father's ghost. Why can't I just be like everyone else? Get drunk without bloating up like a whale afterward, or get high without feeling like I'm going to die?"

"That's ridiculous. Everyone suffers when they overindulge. There are those who own up to it, and those who prefer to brag, that's all."

"Please make the voice stop!" begged Thomas, covering his ears.

"I was just trying to reassure you. No need to be snippy."

But Thomas didn't find it reassuring in the least to hear a dead man speak as if he were in the same room.

"If you would just look over here, you'd see for yourself that your senses aren't playing tricks on you," continued the voice.

Thomas took a deep breath and looked up. In a dark corner, he could make out his father's familiar silhouette gazing warmly at him from the big black leather armchair where he used to like to sit and read. The only word that came to mind was trapped in Thomas's throat: *Dad?*

The anniversary of his father's death, stress about tomorrow's concert, his general state of exhaustion, and a joint he shouldn't have smoked. Maybe all those factors in combination were enough to make him believe something that was unbelievable?

"I'll sleep it off and everything will go back to normal tomorrow," he whispered.

"One day, you'll have to explain to me what you think is 'normal.' Take, for example, the fact that a handsome young man your age—the spitting image of his father, really—who earns his living as a virtuoso pianist, spends the night before a major concert alone, and in his mother's apartment at that. If that's your normal, then you can keep it. Come over here so I can get a good look at you."

But Thomas remained paralyzed by this vision, which was as upsetting to him as it was terrifying.

"Have it your way. I'll try to come over to you, but my movements are still pretty erratic. They should improve over the next few hours. That said, my notion of time isn't what it used to be."

Thomas's eyes widened as he watched his father's form float from the armchair to the mantel, then to the wall across from him, and finally to the corner of the desk.

"Not bad!" his father exclaimed, delighted by his own performance. "I know this must all seem strange, but I promise you're not hallucinating. I really am here, believe you me."

"I feel like I'm talking to Marcel."

"Who's Marcel?" asked Raymond.

"The head lighting engineer at Pleyel. Whenever he critiques my performances, he punctuates his sentence with a 'believe you me, Mr. Thomas.'"

"*Do* you believe him, this lighting engineer?"

"Yes, he's a great music lover."

"But you don't trust your father?"

"Marcel is alive. That may seem like a minor detail to you, but it's a major one to me!" Thomas felt his heart begin to race. "Why am I even answering you? What did I smoke?"

"Look, I figured it would take a while to get through to you, and I'm prepared to be patient, even if we're running out of time. Now, think back to your childhood. When I sat on your bed and told you bedtime stories full of fairies, demons, and creatures with incredible powers from faraway lands, you listened to my voice in the dark, right? And you let yourself believe in my imaginary worlds, didn't you?"

Thomas nodded.

"So, why not believe me now?"

"You're going to stay in this room. I'm going to get up, go into the bathroom, and wash my face, and when I come back, you'll be gone, okay?"

"So stubborn! Aren't you happy to see me?"

Thomas didn't answer. Instead, he gathered his strength to stand up and did what he'd said he would do, carefully closing the office door behind him. After he'd splashed his face with water, he lay down on the couch in the living room, his head still spinning. Then he closed his eyes and fell asleep.

The jingling of keys woke him up. Thomas sat up and saw his mother looking at him tenderly.

"You know you still have a room here, right?" she asked.

"I hadn't planned to stay," he answered as he stretched.

Once he'd shaken his drowsiness, he suddenly turned his head, scanning the room like a hunted animal.

"What's going on?" Jeanne sounded worried.

"Nothing," he answered, rubbing his head. "Did you know that the 'cigarettes' your best friend hides here are actually joints? No wonder she smokes them in secret!"

Jeanne inhaled deeply. "Ah!" she said regretfully. "You may have gotten them from the wrong drawer. Colette's cigarettes were probably in the right-hand drawer after all."

"And in the other?"

"Don't give me that disapproving look. At my age, I can do what I please!"

"Please tell me it's medicinal?"

"There you go jumping to conclusions again. How on earth did I give birth to such a serious son? Where did I go wrong?"

"Normal parents usually have the opposite concern, don't they?"

"Normal parents are boring, admit it. Before I became your mother, I was a sixties girl! We rode in cars without seatbelts, our hair blowing in the wind. We drank, we smoked, and we laughed about everything—especially ourselves—without worrying about offending anyone. We protested for more freedom, not less, and we knew that private lives were best kept private. Some of us died much younger, but in the meantime, we truly lived!"

"What exactly do you put in your joints?" Thomas made an effort to keep his voice calm.

"What do you think? Weed. Very good weed. It's like with wine—you should only get drunk off excellent vintages. It's true, they're a little strong for someone who doesn't often smoke. Your head might be a little fuzzy when you wake up in the morning, but don't worry, it's nothing that would jeopardize your concert. I'm sure my joint isn't what put you in this state you're in, though. What's wrong?"

Thomas told his mother about the strange hallucination he'd had in the next room. She listened thoughtfully, then admitted that maybe she really had rolled too strong a joint.

"So, what did he say?" she asked, sitting beside Thomas as casually as if he had told her he'd run into one of the neighbors on the landing.

"That I wouldn't fall through the window."

"Bizarre . . . What else?"

"Nothing special, except that he'd been a little overprotective when I was a kid."

"A *little*? Your father hovered over you so much, it's a miracle his feet ever touched the ground. But what can you do? He was a doctor and he saw epidemics around every corner. He didn't say anything about me?"

"Mom, it was a hallucination, not a real conversation."

"You never know. I saw him in my dreams once or twice, not long after—"

"Did he talk to you? Could you really see him?" Thomas interrupted, feeling a burst of energy.

"Yes, I saw him, like I said, and yes, he talked to me."

"What did he say to you?"

"That he was sorry, but his excuses meant nothing to me. The nights I saw him, I was a little tipsy, to be honest. Did he seem all right?"

"Same as always, but your question is absurd."

"Did it help you to see him?"

"Not really, no."

"Too bad. Not everyone gets that chance."

"I'd have preferred to skip it, frankly. Although . . . if I hadn't been under the influence, maybe I could have made more of the moment."

"I have a great idea! Come over after your concert and we'll try it again. I have a few things I'd like you to tell him. You can be my messenger." She gave him a conspiratorial glance.

Thomas let out a long sigh. "My mother has just invited me over to smoke weed with her so I can deliver messages to my father's ghost. And you really wonder where you went wrong with my upbringing?"

"Would you prefer I suggest a game of bridge or a macramé class? Go to bed. You have a concert tomorrow. We'll talk about all of this another night. Are Colette and I allowed to come congratulate you in your dressing room after the show, or would that be embarrassing too?"

Thomas kissed his mother on the forehead and left.

He still felt strange as he exited the building, so he decided to take a taxi home. As he walked to the taxi stand, he thought about calling Sophie. He'd never needed her more. He needed to talk to someone who would find the night's events as bizarre as he did, someone who could offer him a little sympathy. He quickly gave up on the idea, though.

He was afraid she'd think he was crazy.

Climbing the five flights of stairs to his small apartment made him feel normal again. His head was clear, and his legs were stable. The drug seemed to have worked its way out of his system, which he found reassuring.

Before heading to bed, Thomas looked around. He walked over to the dormer window and looked up at the sky with a smile.

"If you knew what happened to me tonight, Dad, you would laugh so hard. You scared the shit out of me, but it was nice to see you, even in a weird dream."

Raymond's ghost waited for Thomas to fall asleep, then sat at the foot of his bed.

And as he watched over his son, he smiled.

3

The low rumbling of the crowd rolled through the house, barreling past the backstage curtains. Like an ocean swelling in the wind, anticipation mounted in those who'd come to listen. The orchestra members stood in a single-file line in the hallway that led to the stage. The lights dimmed, and the musicians took their places. They tuned their instruments in a joyful cacophony that hushed the audience. Then it was the pianist's turn to enter the stage.

Colette shot up from her seat and shouted "bravo," further stirring the applause. The conductor climbed onto his platform and turned around to greet Thomas, who stood up from his bench and bowed in return. Marcel was at his post, bathing the Steinway in an almost celestial light.

The conductor lifted his baton. Thomas filled his lungs with air and raised his arms, then delivered the eight measures of slow chords that opened the piece, like a chorus of solemn bells. Then his fingers ran free over the ivory keys, producing a torrent of eighth notes. The violins soon joined him in a murmur that conjured a winter wind gusting across the steppe. Thomas closed his eyes. He was already elsewhere, in Russia, another world, another time, where nothing existed but this romantic fury.

As his hands made their way toward the high notes, Colette jumped up again, this time to get a better view of his agile fingers, which filled her godmother's heart with pride. Jeanne grabbed hold of her and made her sit down.

Performing on a stage gave Thomas a feeling of rapture like nothing else he'd ever known. He was now in a deep discussion with the violins, and the oboes were about to join in. Rachmaninoff had written his Concerto No. 2 while undergoing hypnosis treatment, and the score tells the tale of a rebirth. At the beginning of the first movement, the composer emerges from his torpor, then majestically evokes the pain he has just relived. It was as if Thomas and Rachmaninoff were now one, as if the Russian's ghost had sat down next to him to play, his fingers hovering above Thomas's. It was almost as if . . .

Thomas glanced furtively at the audience and saw his father sitting in the front row, levitating on the knees of a young woman who seemed totally oblivious to his presence.

The conductor showed visible surprise when he heard the pianist skip a few notes. Luckily, he was enough of a virtuoso that he caught up quickly. The orchestra was carrying the melody now, and the piano replied with graceful song. Thomas took advantage of the silence that followed the end of the first movement to wipe his brow. Then the adagio began, slowly, as the flutes and oboes exchanged secrets, the piano spying upon them. Another quick glance—his father had crossed his legs and was smiling proudly. The conductor turned around, intrigued by this second mistake during a wave of rising intensity dominated by the orchestra. Thomas pulled himself together to execute a masterly crescendo and an exquisite staccato.

"Something's wrong," said Colette.

"Yeah . . . with you! Be quiet," whispered Jeanne.

"It's freezing in here, but he's sweating like a pig."

"It's the spotlights," said Jeanne. "You have to stop talking!"

"Look, he keeps shooting strange looks at that woman in the front row. I'm not making it up; surely you can see he's not his usual self."

"You're the one who's not acting normal. He's fine and he's playing like a god!"

"If you say so. I'll leave it at that."

"Shut up and listen."

Their neighbors were visibly annoyed by their conversation. Jeanne smiled apologetically, gesturing at her friend in a manner that suggested she was a few marbles short.

"Go ahead, tell them I'm the crazy one," muttered Colette.

When the third movement started, Thomas left the Russian steppe. The allegro began with a long passage carried by the orchestra, during which the pianist had a difficult time concentrating as he tried desperately not to look at Raymond, who kept crossing and uncrossing his legs. This habit had always annoyed Thomas. Was it even possible for ghosts to be uncomfortable?

A long solo was up next, and if he made even the slightest error, there would be no other instruments to mask his mistake. The intense look the conductor was giving Thomas said much about what awaited him after the concert. He had to hang in there until his backup—the flutes and oboes again—arrived. He had to reach the last measure despite the tingling in his fingers, the drops of sweat pearling on his brow, and a heart shaken by apparitions. He had to stop looking, had to forget the audience and think only of the impending visit from his mother and godmother in his dressing room. This was just another panic attack, like his father had said the night before . . . but no, that was ridiculous.

His father couldn't have said anything, because he'd been dead for five years.

Thomas played the final four chords, triumphantly ending the movement to the audience's delight. Colette leapt out of her seat, again shouting "bravo," a move replicated by the entire audience, which showered the musicians with thunderous applause. The conductor gestured toward the pianist, publicly recognizing his triumph, but when their eyes met, Thomas wasn't fooled—he was furious.

The pianist walked to the edge of the stage and bowed three times to boisterous applause. Then it was the orchestra's turn to stand up and receive its share of praise from the enchanted audience. The curtain fell and the house lights came on.

The conductor put away his baton and came backstage.

"I'm sorry," Thomas explained. "I felt a little unwell."

"I noticed. Nothing serious?"

"Nothing that could jeopardize tomorrow's performance, I promise."

"I hope not," the man replied haughtily as he made his way toward his dressing room.

Thomas went to his own dressing room. He traded his tailcoat and black pants for jeans and a T-shirt, then sat down in the armchair across from the mirror, wondering whether he needed to see a professional. There came a knock at the door, which opened before he could answer. He was expecting to see his mother and godmother, but tonight was full of surprises—he found himself face-to-face with Sophie.

"I wasn't sure you'd pull it off, but you did all right," she said with a smile.

She was stunning in her long black dress. She'd worn her hair up, the way she did when she played, reminding Thomas of the times they'd performed together.

"I didn't know you were in Paris," he said as he got to his feet.

"A coincidence. I'm leaving again tomorrow and wanted to stop by. I considered just texting you when I got back to Rome, but you seemed so bereft when you left the stage."

"Well, it means a lot to me that you came."

"I saw your name on the poster when I walked past this morning. No, that's a lie. I still sometimes follow your tours. Don't ask me why; I have no idea myself."

"Do you want to get dinner somewhere?" he suggested.

"I've met someone, Thomas. Someone who makes me happy. I figured this was as good a time as any to tell you."

"You don't owe me anything."

"I know, but it's better to be open about these things. You aren't angry with me?"

"For being happy? Why would I be angry about that?"

"Because I was also happy with you. You lifted me up without ever truly sweeping me off my feet, held me without truly possessing me, and loved me without desiring me. Does that remind you of anything? Never mind, that's life. I have no regrets."

"*César and Rosalie.* We watched it over and over again when we were performing in Stockholm. It was dubbed in Swedish, but I recited the dialogue for you."

"Without recognizing how much those words hit home."

"Is he a musician, this guy you're seeing?"

"No. Maybe that's why we have a real chance at something. He owns a restaurant in Rome. Not very musical, I know, but you and I are like sailors. We'll drown if we don't have a port to call home."

"Maybe you're right."

She walked over to him, gave him a tight hug, and gently touched his cheek.

"You deserve to be happy, too, Thomas. When you meet her, don't let her leave like you did with me. Find the courage to actually want to love her."

She kissed his forehead, turned to leave, and then looked back from the doorway. "If I'm not mistaken, you skipped a few notes in the adagio."

And with that she was gone.

Thomas waited a few seconds, then returned to his chair facing the mirror, and to his thoughts.

"A masterful display of feminine genius!" exclaimed his father as he appeared in the mirror. "She must have really planned out her revenge. I have to hand it to her: It was a consummate performance. Such cruelty! And the way she touched your cheek with that hint of maternal affection. Vicious *and* talented." He mimed applause. "Checkmate, buddy, she got you good."

"Would you please just leave me alone?" groaned Thomas.

"After what I just witnessed? No way. I had no idea I'd neglected your emotional education to such a degree. I hope you'll remember at least part of the lesson she's just taught you. It took her just two minutes and a few sentences to let you know you're nothing but a memory. She came right up to the net to let you hope there might still be something between you, and then she delivered the smash—you missed your chance at happiness, which of course she embodied. There was no way you could hit that one back. Magnificent, I must say. Then, not satisfied with having brought you to your knees, she added insult to injury with her mention of your mistake. A real dragon!"

"Are you done?"

"I said everything I had to say."

"You're the reason I messed up my notes."

"What do you mean? I wasn't the one onstage."

"No, you were in the front row . . . on some woman's lap, surprise, surprise. That wasn't distracting at all."

"I don't have much time, so don't blame me for using some of it to hear my son play."

"You had something better to do?"

"I could have spent my evening at the Lido," his father said, speaking of the famous cabaret on the Champs-Élysées, "and taken advantage of my abilities to wander the halls unseen."

"You can't be here in this mirror. You can't be talking to me. You can't be real because you're dead!"

"You have a choice: Either you continue to deny what's happening here, and we waste precious time on useless speculation, or you admit that sometimes things happen without any rational explanation. When I was a kid, which, sadly, was in the middle of the last century, people said it was impossible to transplant a human heart; yet, now it's done regularly. And before that, they said humans would never fly, but now San Francisco is just eleven hours away. Do you want more examples?"

"But ghosts don't exist!"

"Well, then, the Tibetans, the Chinese, the Japanese, and the Scottish, and all the other civilizations that have worshiped their ancestors for centuries, are bumbling idiots. Thank goodness you, Thomas, know the truth."

There was another knock at the door. Thomas asked in an annoyed voice who it was.

"It's your mother and Colette," whispered Raymond. "Who else could it be? Don't say anything about my being here, of course. I'll go now and come back when they're gone."

Thomas stood and opened the door. Colette entered first; Jeanne slipped in behind her.

"You were amazing!" exclaimed his godmother. "We just came to give you a kiss and then we'll let you rest, unless you want to get a drink with two old ladies. Your mother keeps telling everyone who'll listen that I'm going senile."

"You'll exhaust him, Colette," Jeanne said with a sigh.

"Ah, well. At least I made it ten minutes without getting scolded."

Thomas hugged his mother.

"The audience was over the moon," she said.

"Forget the moon," Thomas replied. "I played poorly. I'm lucky the orchestra was there to cover for me."

"See, just like I said!" Colette exclaimed triumphantly. "I noticed you weren't your usual self, but don't worry, the audience was none the wiser. Your own mother didn't even realize it. Who were you staring daggers at in the front row?"

"Someone who disappeared from my life a long time ago," he said, staring at his reflection in the mirror.

Jeanne and Colette exchanged curious glances. Jeanne took her friend by the arm and pushed her toward the door.

"Let's leave him be. I can see my boy is tired. I still know him better than you do."

She waved to Thomas as she dragged Colette away. Colette blew him a kiss as she left.

Thomas heard his godmother grumbling in the hallway, and then there was silence.

The mirror reflected nothing but his own features. His mother wasn't wrong—his face was ashen. Thomas hung up his stage clothes, grabbed his leather bag, turned out the lights in his dressing room, and left.

He ran into Marcel backstage and nodded good night, then walked out the stage door that led to the street. There, he found his father sitting on the hood of a car, his legs crossed.

"I would have loved to take you to dinner, but . . . well, I can at least keep you company if you want to grab a bite."

"What I really want is to be alone."

"Crazy, isn't it?" replied his father as he placed his arm around Thomas's shoulder.

"You're telling me!"

"What am I telling you?" asked a man who, at that very moment, had been passing Thomas on the sidewalk.

"Nothing. I wasn't talking to you."

"There's no one else on the street," the man pointed out. "And I don't like your tone."

"Forget it," Thomas said, annoyed.

"Why should *I* forget it? You're the one who just loudly accused me of telling you something a moment ago."

Thomas stared at the man. "Maybe there's some sort of toxic gas or pollution in the air that's making everyone a little crazy," he suggested.

"You should watch your manners, young man. You're the only one who's crazy. You were just talking to yourself."

Thomas shrugged and kept walking. When he turned his head to the side, he saw his father, who wasn't even trying to hide his amusement.

"You think this is funny?"

"Where's your sense of humor? It was like a Raymond Devos sketch."

"Who?"

"He was a stand-up comedian who . . . Oh, never mind. You're too young to know him."

"Why are you here? Why can I hear and see you?"

"I'm guessing just answering 'because' won't cut it. But I'd rather explain when we get to your place. That way you can sit down and listen closely. We need to talk."

"And then you'll leave me alone?"

"Is seeing me again really so terrible?"

"That's not what I meant. Losing you wasn't exactly easy. You'd taken up so much space in my life. Mom said it would take time, that I'd go through different stages of grief, but I didn't realize how intense that process would be."

"Did your mother talk to you about me much after my death?"

"You're aware that your question is ridiculous, right?"

"Actually, awareness is about all I've got going for me in my current state. What do you mean, I took up 'so much space'? Did you feel that I overshadowed you somehow?"

He called the last line as Thomas was walking away.

Thomas pushed open the door to his building. When he looked up the stairwell, he saw his father leaning over the railing on the top floor.

"I thought ghosts were supposed to drag along a ball and chain!" he said with a sigh, seeing him up there.

He left his bag in the entryway of his apartment and went straight to the fridge for a beer before collapsing onto his couch.

His father sat down in the armchair across from him.

"You have no idea how much your need to constantly cross and uncross your legs bothers me."

"It's not my fault, my legs are too long," his father said. "I've never known what to do with them. Did I have any other habits that annoyed you?"

"Why don't we get back to the purpose of your little visit? Is there perhaps some aspect of your life that lacks closure?"

"Don't be rude, Thomas. I'm still your father."

"And given the way you're haunting me, I'm not likely to forget it."

"I came back because I have a big favor to ask of you. If you accept, I promise I'll leave you alone. But before we talk about that, there are some things I have to tell you about my life. Unless, of course, you're worried that it will cast too big of a shadow."

When Thomas didn't answer, Raymond looked upset. "Why won't you say anything? Why are you so cold and distant? Are you mad at me about something? Do you think I didn't love you enough?"

"You set such impossibly high standards," Thomas told him. "I could never live up to them. You were this famous surgeon who saved lives, and I just play music."

"What are you talking about? You make people's lives better. You should have seen the faces in the audience tonight. I was overwhelmed with pride. Sure, I saved a few lives in my day, but in my profession, there's no applause when you leave the operating room. No one hands you flowers when the symphony of scalpels is over."

"Look who's become a poet."

"One of the benefits of death," his father replied, his old confidence back.

"All right, I'll hear you out. But then you have to let me sleep. I'm exhausted. Okay? You promise?"

"I promise." Raymond pretended to spit on the ground to seal the deal. "Now, let's see. Where should I begin?"

"By explaining how exactly you're here?"

"Sorry, I'm not allowed to talk about that. It was the one condition for obtaining this short leave."

"'Leave,' like in the army?"

"No, but sure, you can think of it like that."

"So, you took a leave from the afterlife to come see me?" Thomas broke into a fit of laughter.

"Are you done making fun of me?"

"This is unbelievable! I'm talking to my father's ghost in the middle of the night . . . Go on, please. Continue. I have a feeling this is just the beginning." He wiped his eyes with the back of his hand.

"I need your help to do something that will determine my fate for all eternity."

"Of course! It all makes sense now. You were sent back to earth to save humanity, just like you used to save your patients. And like any good Don Quixote, you need a Sancho—and you thought of me."

"Stop messing around. This is urgent."

"What can possibly be urgent when you're dead?"

"You'll find out one day. A long time from now, I hope. Now, are you going to let me finish or keep interrupting me?"

Thomas agreed to stay quiet. He was convinced he was trapped in a strange dream from which he would eventually awake. This idea comforted him as he listened to his father.

"I'll begin with saying that your mother and I hadn't been close in some time . . ."

"That's not exactly breaking news. You left home ten years before you died."

"I'm talking about another time. Not long after you were born. By that time in our relationship, our life together had become more like an arrangement between friends."

"Great. If I had a therapist, a disclosure like that would guarantee them a very comfortable retirement."

"It wasn't like that before you were born," his father said, ignoring this comment. "We truly loved each other then, but we grew apart. It was partly my fault."

"'Partly' how?"

"I met another woman."

"You had an affair, that's your big revelation? You were able to seduce anyone who crossed your path, so that's hardly a surprise."

"You've got me all wrong. I was a flirt, yes, but hardly a womanizer. And besides, I never got to live out my great love, which may be why I'm unable to let it go."

"It's that anesthesiologist at the hospital who always followed you around making eyes at you, isn't it? I always suspected there was something going on between the two of you."

"You remember Violette?"

"Every time I visited you at work, she stroked my forehead as if I was a poodle and swooned, telling me I was the spitting image of you."

"Well, it's not her. We did have a brief dalliance, but nothing of consequence."

"Are you speaking for yourself or for Mom?"

"Judge me all you want with your therapist once you get one. In the meantime, let me continue."

"The green-eyed pediatrician, then?"

"Stop it! I didn't meet Camille at the hospital."

"'Camille.' Got it. So, where did you meet?"

"Do you remember the seaside town where we spent all our summers?"

"You mean where I spent my days hunting for clams in the sludgy sand, riding the merry-go-round, going on pony rides, always losing at mini-golf? The picnics Mom packed for the beach, walks by the lighthouse, the crepe stand by the port, and the games of Monopoly when it rained? I'd have to have a pretty bad case of amnesia to forget that kind of monotony."

"That's not fair. You had the time of your life on those vacations."

"Did you ever ask me, even once, if I was really having fun?"

Raymond studied his son for a moment, then continued his story. "That's where we met."

"Thrilled to hear it. What's that got to do with me?"

"Well, let's just say that the clam hunts, the merry-go-round, the riding club, and the crepe stand all provided opportunities for us to be together. You were the pretext for all our dates."

"You used me as a cover? That's disgusting."

"Oh, get your mind out of the gutter! We didn't do anything wrong, Thomas. We loved each other from afar, for your sake. Every now and then, we would hold hands discreetly, making our hearts race. Other times, we would brush up against each other, just barely. But mostly, we exchanged glances and stories, nothing more."

"Spare me the details!" Thomas protested.

"You're not five years old anymore. Won't you at least try to listen to me without making this all about you?"

"This is turning my entire world upside down. Do you want to know what I actually *did* enjoy about our summers under those depressing gray skies? Unlike the rest of the year, when your patients and your operating room took up every moment of your time, I had you to myself. We spent time together, just the two of us. So, I'm not exactly thrilled to learn that those hours you carved out for me were, in fact, just a pretext to see your mistress."

"Camille wasn't my mistress. She was much more than that. And did you ever ask yourself if *I* was having fun, if I was happy, or even just okay?"

"I was a kid!" Thomas cried.

"And then you grew up—and I nearly died of loneliness!"

"What about Mom?"

"It wasn't your mother's fault. It wasn't mine, either. It was love at first sight, Thomas. Some things can't be explained," Raymond said quietly.

"And one of those things is talking to a ghost!" Thomas shouted. "I'm going to bed. Feel free to haunt whoever you like, wherever you like. All I ask is that you stay away from the foot of my bed."

"If that's what you want. We'll continue this conversation tomorrow. The concert must have worn you out. It wasn't the right time to tell you all that."

Thomas stood up and walked to his bedroom. Before he went in, he turned back toward his father and gave him an angry look.

"We won't talk about this tomorrow, because we're not talking about this now. I'm simply having a nightmare that's populated by all my anxieties: Sophie, you, making mistakes onstage at the Salle Pleyel, dirty looks from my conductor, Marcel's disappointment. In reality, I'm still at Mom's house, sleeping on the couch in the living room, and when I wake up, none of this will have happened. It will still be the anniversary of your death, I won't have seen Sophie, and my concert won't have happened yet.

"And I'll still have only good memories of summer vacations with my father."

4

Thomas had a hard time waking up. He opened his eyes, still heavy with sleep, and realized that his ringing phone had disturbed his dreams. He reached half-heartedly for his smartphone and looked at the screen. There was no point in rejecting the call—his mother would keep at it until he finally answered.

She poured a flood of words into his ear. Fortunately, his mother's voice was soothing. He put the phone down on his pillow and listened, occasionally mumbling a reply.

"Were you able to get some rest?"

"Mm-hm."

"I'm sorry you felt so bad after smoking. I shouldn't have joked about it. Everyone reacts differently. Your father always loved to make fun of my allergies, claiming they were all in my head. What if they are? Whether they originate in my head or my blood, the result's the same, isn't it?"

"Mm-hm."

"The big one for me, sweetheart, is garlic. Just a hint of it in a dish and I can't sleep all night. Or rather, my stomach can't."

"Mm-hm."

"You looked so awful, I felt guilty. I hope the effects have all worn off. If they haven't, you can try the usual hangover remedies. There's nothing like tomato juice when you wake up to get it out of your system. Lemon juice works well too. In any case, as sick as you looked, you were still very handsome."

"Mm-hm."

"Your godmother and I will attend the concert tonight, but I'll make sure she doesn't embarrass you. And don't worry, we'll be happy with whatever seats you give us. Don't forget to leave the tickets at the box office. Two, of course!"

"Mm-hm."

"I just realized I'm repeating myself since I already told you Colette was coming with me, or I guess I'm coming with her. We'll see you afterward, in your dressing room. I'm so proud of you, you know. I'll never be able to say that enough. What time is it? Only eight. Oh God, still early. I'll let you get back to sleep. Love you, sweetheart, see you tonight."

Thomas let his phone drop onto the rug. He opened his eyes and looked around his room. To his relief, it was filled with silence and golden morning light. The delightful solitude awakened his senses.

Since his mother had asked for tickets for tonight, that meant she hadn't attended the concert the night before. And that meant the night he remembered had never happened. No concert, no mistakes, no Sophie, and, above all, no ghost. Before he could fully rejoice, he still needed to check. He called out to his father.

"Dad? Dad, are you there? If you're hiding somewhere to scare me, it's not funny."

A memory pushed its way to the surface. The game he'd played with his father from the time he was little—they would take turns hiding and trying to scare the other by jumping out at him. The game had started around when he was six and continued until the end of his dad's life. They would hide behind trees at the end of the school day, in a school locker room, in the foyer of one or the other's building, in elevators, backstage, even at the hospital, where Thomas once managed to sneak into his father's office with the help of his secretary. Almost anywhere was fair game—except for the stage and the operating room. Those two were off-limits.

"Dad?" he called out once again as he threw open the door to his closet. It contained nothing but a suitcase and a coat.

Satisfied that he was alone, he turned on the coffee maker and sat down at his kitchen table to have breakfast, feeling a little depressed.

Later, in the shower, Thomas felt the impulse to talk to someone about the dream. Perhaps if he shared the details, he would become free of it.

Sylvain was a friendly longtime acquaintance, almost a real friend, who was also a psychiatrist and a music lover. Thomas had given him tickets to several concerts. Maybe he could ask a favor in return.

He called Sylvain and invited him to lunch. Sylvain was no fool—he said he could tell from Thomas's voice that he needed to talk, not split a steak. A brasserie wasn't the ideal location for getting whatever it was off his chest. A love affair gone wrong? "Psychiatrists aren't couples' counselors, you know," he said.

"It's something else," Thomas assured him. "And you're right. A quiet place would be better. What I have to tell you is truly insane."

Sounding intrigued, Sylvain told him to come to his office later that morning.

Thomas chose an armchair instead of the couch.

"Even if this isn't a real appointment, you still can't tell anyone what I say, right?"

"I'm already discreet by nature, my friend. But yes, whatever you say here today will never leave this room. Now, if you want me to help you, you have to tell me why you're here."

Thomas told Sylvain about everything he'd been through—or thought he'd been through—in great detail.

The doctor listened to him for an hour, taking notes but never interrupting. When Thomas finally finished, Sylvain urged him to try to put words to the question that had brought him to his office.

"None of what I've just told you makes any sense, but it seemed completely real. Do you think just one joint could have damaged my neurons so badly, enough to make me go crazy?"

"Don't ever use the word 'crazy' in a psychiatrist's office. It's taboo," Sylvain told him. "No one is crazy. Everyone has his or her own perception of reality, because reality is, as you may already know, subjective. When you play for an audience, for example, you're physically present onstage, but your consciousness is elsewhere. Your mind projects itself as if in a dream, exactly like it does when you're sleeping. When a dream is still very present upon waking, we have to try to separate the real from the imaginary. The dream haunts us until it fades."

"What day is it?"

"Saturday."

"Then yesterday was real!"

"Friday always comes before Saturday, my friend, that's a fact! But maybe you experienced it in a sort of hypnotic state. That happens to a lot of people. Sometimes it only lasts a moment, like the feeling of déjà vu that troubles us all; other times it lasts a little longer. Even a small emotional shock can provoke it. Our brain chemistry is capable of far more than we suspect."

"Do you think a psychotropic drug could have long-lasting effects?"

"Depends on the drug. Your joint certainly didn't cause your problem. Your high comes from a much stronger and more tenacious drug: Judeo-Christian guilt."

"Hmm . . ."

"During this episode, did your father reproach you for anything?"

Thomas nodded.

"I suspected as much. Tell me more."

"I don't know what he said exactly. Something about me never having asked if he was happy, I think."

"You see, talking about it is already helping the memory to fade. Who else came to you in the dream? We'll talk more about your father later."

"Sophie, like I said."

"Sophie, whom you're no longer with because you were unable to commit to a real relationship."

"Yeah, well, I guess," Thomas mumbled.

"Even though she was ready for a relationship and wanted to be with you."

Another nod.

"Who else?"

"My mother and my godmother."

"Two women you love unconditionally, whom you can never push away. Two women you've never been in competition with, the way you have with your father."

"I don't see what that's got to do with anything."

"I do. Did anyone else talk to you?"

"No, no one. Well, except this guy in the street who didn't make much sense. He gave my dad a good laugh, though. He alluded to some comedian I'm apparently too young to know about."

"Young or not, you're magnificently astute in the way you used this faceless stranger to evoke the wounds of childhood. A representation of inattentive adults who never really hear what children say. You see where I'm going with this? Do you feel better?"

"Maybe, though I'm not totally convinced."

"One more question, then, to reassure you. Are you absolutely sure you didn't leave anyone out?"

"Are you talking about the conductor?"

"The conductor! The physical embodiment of authority in all its glory. The only person you see as capable of judging and validating your talents. I remember our school days well enough to recall how you struggled with authority. We're getting closer now, but we're still missing someone. And it's hardly a coincidence that you've left him out."

"Honestly, Sylvain, I can't think of anyone else."

"Keep thinking."

"Marcel?"

"Exactly. Marcel, the lighting engineer. The one who turns the lights on and off and ends his sentences with 'believe you me.'"

"What does Marcel have to do with anything?"

"Marcel is your conscience. He's your ego and your superego, which are in constant conflict. The fact that this nightmare seemed so real and just happened to fall on the anniversary of your father's death signals that it's a reminder from your conscience. It's telling you, 'My dear Thomas, you haven't finished grieving for your father.' Even if Marcel says 'believe you me,' super-Marcel tells you not to believe him, because you still have a long way to go."

"Marcel is telling me all that?"

"Yes," the psychiatrist answered calmly.

"If that's what you really think, then I believe you."

"You see, you've come full circle. You believe me, you believe Marcel, you believe everyone, but now what you have to do is believe in yourself and accept that your father isn't here anymore to protect you. You also have to accept your own mortality, and above all, you have to stop being afraid to commit to the next Sophie. And now, as much as I'd like to spend the whole day with you, I have patients with much more complicated situations than yours. Have fun tonight. You won't make any mistakes, your mother will be delighted, and neither Sophie nor your father's ghost will haunt you."

"What do I owe you?" asked Thomas as he stood up.

"Lunch sometime. But if you could get me tickets to the Verdi concert at Garnier at the end of the month, you'd have my eternal gratitude."

Sylvain walked Thomas to the door of his office and patted his shoulder, repeating that everything would be back to normal soon, if it wasn't already.

Back on the street, Thomas felt lighter on his feet. To banish the last hint of doubt, he took out his phone and called his ex-girlfriend.

"Thomas?" she asked, surprised.

"I'm sorry, I don't want to bother you, especially if you're with someone, but I have an important question to ask and it won't take long. Did you come to see me in my dressing room after the concert last night? I can't figure out if it was part of a nightmare or if it was real. I'm leaning toward nightmare, even though you seemed real—I mean, I thought you did. You looked stunning, but what you said was so surreal that I haven't been sure since I woke up this morning. Especially since your visit wasn't even the strangest thing that happened in my surreal day. But it was part of it, and I just wanted to make sure. You understand?"

There was a long silence, and Thomas wondered if she had hung up on him.

"Sophie?"

"I'm here." She sighed. "You know what, Thomas? Maybe I made a huge mistake in letting you go. I should have been more patient, because guys as twisted and wonderful as you don't come along every day. Honestly, I'm still not sure if I should feel relief, or regret."

Then she hung up.

Thomas realized she hadn't answered his question. Maybe he hadn't asked it clearly enough?

As he kept walking, he decided it would be best not to think about any of it anymore. Better to forget his hypnotic day, as Sylvain had called it, and focus on tonight's concerto.

He took advantage of a few rays of sunshine on the terrace of Les Deux Magots, where he ordered a salad. When the waiter returned to the kitchen, Thomas went to buy a paper from the newsstand next door. He then returned to his place and thanked the couple next to him for watching his jacket and bag. He was enjoying his beer when he heard a sigh behind him.

"Psychiatrists are so full of shit! If your conscience is as weighty as good old Marcel, your thoughts must be heavy indeed. Ego and superego. Absolute nonsense."

Thomas refused to answer his father. He paid for his lunch and put on his jacket, then picked up his newspaper and casually crossed Boulevard Saint-Germain to get to the taxi stand. He climbed into a Škoda and asked the driver to take him to the Salle Pleyel.

The car was driving down Rue Bonaparte when Raymond appeared in the passenger seat and turned around to talk to Thomas.

"First of all, you and I were never in competition with one another. And second, you never had trouble with authority in school. I should know since I attended all the parent-teacher meetings."

"No, you didn't. Mom did," corrected Thomas under his breath.

"Fair enough, but still—the 'wounds of childhood'? Let's just summon the lesions of adolescence while we're at it! And the scars of old age too—I know all about that one, from tangible life experience. My profession was pretty tangible too. When you're operating on someone, there's nothing subjective about it. Either you cut or you don't, and then you sew them back up, that's it."

Thomas started to hum while he looked out the window, like a child refusing to listen.

"Would you like me to turn on the radio?" The driver looked a bit unnerved.

"No, it's fine," Thomas answered. "I prefer silence, thanks."

"Was that directed at me?" asked his father.

"Who else would it be directed at? Didn't you hear Sylvain say I hadn't completed the grieving process? And by the way . . . your criticism of psychiatrists is pathetic."

"Have you got some kind of psychological problem?" asked the driver, a hint of worry in his voice.

"See what you've gotten me into?" Thomas complained to his father.

"I didn't get you into anything," protested the driver. "You're the one talking to me."

"Who was calling who this morning in your apartment? 'Dad? Dad?' I had given you your space so you could get a good night's sleep. Your mother's the one who woke you up, not me."

"She woke me up from a nightmare that I thought was over!"

"We're pretty close to Pompidou hospital. I can drop you off, if you'd like," offered the driver. "We're less than ten minutes away. There's no traffic."

"Thanks, but I don't need to go to the hospital."

"If you say so, but you don't exactly seem well. It's your call. But no mental breakdowns in my taxi, okay?"

"I'm sorry, I was practicing my lines for a play."

"Oh, that makes sense." The driver sighed in relief. "What play? My wife loves the theater."

"*A Father's Past.* A complicated story about a father-son relationship."

"Go ahead, joke about it," Raymond cut in. "Mock me all you want. But if you wanted to kill your father, the way psychiatrists always suggest, you missed your chance. I'm already dead."

"Hilarious."

"Oh, even better, I love comedy," said the driver. "I find dramatic plays depressing, but my wife loves them, and I love my wife, so what's a guy to do? Who's in the play with you?"

"I don't have a good answer to that."

"Is it a one-man show?"

"Sort of, yes."

After that, Thomas remained silent. His father kept his eyes glued to the road, his arms crossed and a frown on his face.

When the car stopped in front of the Salle Pleyel, the driver turned to Thomas and asked for an autograph as he handed him his change.

His father followed him to the stage door.

"All right, I'll stay here," he said. "I'll keep away from the concert, to avoid distracting you. But you have to agree to listen to me afterward. I really need you. You're my son. You're the only person I can count on, and time is running out."

Thomas felt moved by his father's distress. He'd never seen such sadness in his father's eyes before. Raymond was a proud man, the kind to hide his emotions and always insist he was fine. And his son knew better than anyone that Raymond was not fine now.

"All right," Thomas said. "Meet me here after the concert and we'll go to my place. This time I'll listen."

Raymond wrapped his arms around Thomas, who could feel his father's tenderness in the gesture. He hesitated for a moment, then returned the hug, which filled him with a feeling of satisfaction that was as strange as it was welcome.

The driver, who was watching from a distance, put his foot on the gas. "That's actors for you," he said. "Real pieces of work. Every last one of them."

5

His father was waiting outside the stage door, his back against a lamppost. Thomas stopped to watch him for a moment. Raymond was wearing his usual blazer, tweed pants, and polished loafers. He looked up and smiled warmly at his son.

"How did it go?" he asked.

"Not a single mistake," replied Thomas.

"How's your mother?"

"How do you know she came if you stayed out here?"

"I saw her go in," Raymond stammered.

"Okay . . . Let's head home. I'm tired."

Thomas walked to the Metro station.

"We're not taking a taxi?" Raymond asked.

"Do you think I'm made of money?"

"I'd happily foot the bill, but unfortunately my account has been closed," his father joked. "I hate the Metro, but since we've no choice . . ."

Despite the late hour, their subway car was packed. Thomas changed lines at the Villiers station and managed to find a seat before the train filled up at Saint-Lazare. His father stood next to him without any need to hold on.

"Get up," whispered Raymond, glancing toward an older woman swaying on her frail legs.

Thomas jumped out of his seat and offered it to her. "I'm sorry," he said, "I wasn't paying attention."

The woman smiled at him and sat down, visibly relieved.

"Thanks for saying something," Thomas whispered to his father. "I honestly hadn't noticed her."

"Who cares about an old lady with blocked arteries—she's already got one foot in the grave, and I would know. But did you see the stunning young woman sitting across from you? Thanks to me, she noticed you, or at least your chivalrous gesture. With a smile like yours and a single word, you could have her wrapped around your finger."

Thomas didn't respond, wanting to avoid looking like a nut job in a crowded subway train. His father looked disappointed when the young woman got off at the Opéra station, brushing against Thomas as she reached the doors.

"You *really* need my help. And at Opéra, no less—she may have been a ballerina!"

"And if she'd gotten off at Saint-Lazare, would you have assumed she was a train station manager?" asked Thomas.

"Excuse me?" said the older woman.

"Nothing, I'm just talking to myself," he apologized.

"Don't worry, I do that all the time."

Raymond shook his head in exasperation.

When he got home, Thomas dropped his things on the floor and collapsed onto the couch with a long sigh.

"You could at least pretend. Are you really not happy to see me again?" Raymond asked.

"Of course I am."

"But to admit that is to also admit that I'm really here."

"The weeks and months after you died were hard. I was just starting to get used to not having you around."

"I understand that."

"No, you don't. When I lost you, I fell into a dark depression. Could you hear me all those times when I poured my heart out to that photo of you?"

Raymond smiled tenderly at Thomas but didn't answer.

"Where were you during all that time?"

"I don't know. Dying wasn't easy for me, either; leaving you was harder."

"What's it like in the afterlife?"

"Thomas," said his father in a grave tone, "I'm not allowed to tell you anything, and even if I was, I doubt I'd be able to explain it. Let's just say it's different."

"Are you happy there?"

"I don't have arthritis anymore, so there's that. But with your help? I could be genuinely happy."

"With my help?"

"Yes, the favor I mentioned."

"About that woman?"

"Camille. I'd be grateful if you could refer to her by her name." His father sat down on the upright piano. "When I think of all the things she and I missed out on, all the time we have to make up for . . ."

"Yes, of course, thanks to me. You mentioned that."

"It wasn't just because of you. Such choices weren't considered acceptable back then."

"So, in fact, you really are here to haunt me. I think Sylvain underestimated the extent of the damage you've done."

"Stop worrying about what that charlatan thinks. You told him you saw a ghost, and he offered some casual, off-the-cuff diagnosis without even bothering to examine you. Would it have killed him to take your blood pressure? If a patient—no, a friend—had told me something like that, I would have sent him off for a series of tests immediately."

"Is that your professional medical opinion? You think I should go to the emergency room?" Thomas asked.

"It's my professional medical opinion, yes, but about your psychiatrist friend. You're perfectly healthy. Nothing wrong with *your* head. Do you really think I haven't been studying you since I came back? You look tired, sure, but no one your age who doesn't wear themselves out is really living. When I was thirty-five I worked eighty-hour weeks, and it didn't kill me."

"Well, it did eventually."

"A little respect, please. I happen to think I held up pretty well. I'm telling you, you're fine. If you go to the emergency room and tell them you're having little chats with your father's ghost, you'll end up getting checked into Sainte-Anne Psychiatric Hospital."

That was probably true, Thomas thought. His father seemed to take his silence as encouragement to continue.

"Camille has just died." Raymond lowered his head as if suddenly plunged into a flood of grief. "What do you have to say about that?"

"What do you want me to say? I'm sorry for her, but it's not like I knew her."

"A kind word would have been nice. In any case, now that she and I are both on the other side, we've decided to tie the proverbial knot, so we'll always be a couple."

"Good for you, but what does any of that have to do with me? Other than the fact that when Mom dies, I won't be able to console myself by picturing the two of you together."

"Oh, don't be a hypocrite. You were the first to say our divorce came as a relief."

"Fine, but how do I fit in to your eternal plans?"

"Well, it's just—if Camille and I are to spend eternity together, our ashes need to be united."

"Excuse me?"

"Or, mixed together, if you prefer. All you have to do is pour the contents of one urn into the other and give it a good shake. Once you scatter them all, we'll be free and together forever. Now, don't look at me like that; I'm not the one who came up with the rules of the universe. Being buried side by side could also have worked, but it's too late for me on that front. And anyway, why should we settle for a tiny studio when we could have a huge terrace with an ocean view?"

"What's this studio you're talking about?"

"A grave or coffin, naturally! And who knows who we'd have as neighbors. No, Camille and I want to spend our eternity outdoors. It's not like I'm asking you for the moon here."

"What exactly *are* you asking me for?" Thomas held his breath.

"Something as easy as pie. Camille's funeral will take place in a few days. You simply go to the ceremony, wait for her to be cremated afterward, then briefly borrow her urn so you can pour in the contents of mine. That's it!"

"You forgot to mention giving it a good shake," Thomas deadpanned.

"That goes without saying."

"So, to sum up, you want me to attend the funeral of a woman I didn't know but who was your mistress, and then steal what's left of her out from under the nose of her family."

"You've got it!"

"I'd rather you'd asked me to get you the moon. It certainly would be easier. Where is this funeral, by the way?"

"In San Francisco."

"Naturally." Thomas sighed.

"Why did you say 'naturally' in that weird tone of voice?"

"Now my tone is weird?"

"Very. Quite strange."

"I guess it would have been too easy for the funeral to take place in Pantin or at Père-Lachaise Cemetery."

"Not necessarily. But I had nothing to do with it. I'm not the one who sent her to live so far away. Despite our exceptional discretion, her husband figured out what we were up to and was careful to keep us away from each other. He arranged to get a job transfer to California, choosing—rather selfishly, if you ask me—to uproot his family."

"I actually think it's pretty brave of him, leaving everything behind for love. Traveling to the other side of the world to protect his marriage."

"Not for love, out of jealousy!"

"Why did his wife go with him if she loved you so much?"

"Because of her daughter. The same reason I stayed in Paris for you."

"Oh, right. For a moment, I forgot that I ruined your life."

"I never said that, and I didn't think it, either. In any case, keeping us apart didn't change the way she felt."

"How do you know that?"

"After she left, I decided I needed to live with the choice I'd made. I let her go because I couldn't leave you and your mother. I refused to torment Camille, so I kept quiet for months. I felt the pain of that silence every single day, and even more so when we were on summer vacation. If Camille had fallen back in love with her husband, she wouldn't have started writing to me, and we wouldn't have continued to correspond for the next twenty years. But she did, and we did."

"You told some other woman all about our lives?"

"I told her about mine. The letters were mostly about me, but not entirely, it's true."

"What about her husband? What did he do out there in California? No, you know what, don't even answer that. I don't know why I'm asking."

"He went there as an aeronautics engineer, but he played the tech boom in Silicon Valley just right and ended up a multimillionaire. I find it all a bit gauche, but to each his own, right?"

"Did you know him?"

"Of course I did. The situation was all terribly banal. We couples ran into each other all the time on vacation, so we ended up becoming friendly. We had dinner together on occasion, and we even shared a babysitter, who watched you and their daughter at the same time. Right up until Camille and I understood that we had fallen for each other."

"Those must have been fun evenings. Two lovers and two emotionally abandoned spouses—one of them Mom—all at the same table."

"Wait until you've lived a little more before you judge me. Would you believe me if I told you that my relationship with Camille was always perfectly chaste?"

"Why wouldn't I believe you? You've told me far more unbelievable things than that."

"Listen to me, Thomas! If her husband scatters her ashes before you get there, it'll all be over."

"What will be over?"

"Us. Camille and me. She couldn't be my partner in life, but I want her to be my partner in death. I can't do that without your help."

"Have you asked Camille what she thinks about all this? Do you have any idea what *she* wants?"

"You really think that, after twenty years of exchanging letters with her, I don't know what she wants?"

"Did you keep them?"

"They're in a wooden box next to my urn."

"That's a charming image. Where is your urn, anyway?"

"Hidden behind some books on the top shelf of the bookcase at your mom's place."

"So, you really *were* there when I saw you in the office, then."

"Yes. Well, what's left of me."

"And you're telling me that Mom kept the letters from the woman who stole her husband?"

"Camille didn't steal anything—I stayed with your mother. She and I remained good friends. We could count on each other, whatever the circumstances. The box is locked, and your mother is very smart. She knows better than to try and open it."

"I understand now," Thomas whispered.

"What do you understand?"

"Why Mom refused to scatter your ashes. I thought it was because she couldn't bear to let you go, but she really was just respecting your wishes. You told her that you were leaving her everything, and all you asked in return was that she keep them. You even made a dark joke, saying that if your presence bothered her, she could store you in the basement. That made the lawyer laugh. So, were you planning this all along?"

"Not really. I couldn't imagine that someday I'd ask you to do me this favor. I certainly didn't know what lay ahead for me. But Camille and I always dreamed of reuniting in another life, of spending eternity together. Will you think about it tonight? About making our dream come true? Go to bed now, and give me your answer tomorrow. Don't oversleep—we're running out of time."

"I doubt I'll sleep late. I don't know if I'll sleep at all after everything you've just told me. Thanks for that."

"Would you rather play poker, then?" Raymond asked cheerfully. "You loved playing poker as a kid. I would always let you win, because you fell into a black rage every time you lost. Now that you're a man, you won't find it so easy to beat me."

"Can you actually hold the cards?" Thomas asked, surprised.

"No. Good point. You could play solitaire, though. I'll sit across from you. A fantastic idea! Instead of playing against each other, we'll play as a team."

Thomas studied his father with amusement.

"Is this little charm offensive supposed to convince me to do what you want?"

"Son, when I was alive, I was constantly trying to charm you into one thing or convince you of another. But if there's one thing my experience as a parent taught me, it's just how little control I had."

Raymond placed his hand on his son's shoulder. Strangely, Thomas could feel his presence. A glance passed between them that said everything words could not.

Thomas went to grab the deck of cards from his desk drawer. He placed one face up, then six more face down in a row. Sitting across from him, Raymond watched and occasionally made a suggestion.

The evening continued in this way until Thomas's head dropped to the table and he drifted off to sleep. Watching with a mischievous glint in his eye, Raymond whispered in his son's ear that he would be more comfortable in bed.

With that, Thomas rose and walked all the way to his bedroom, still wholly and deeply asleep.

6

As the morning light filtered in through the dormer windows, Thomas squinted and wondered briefly where he was. His memory of the night before was muddled.

Standing in front of the kitchen sink, Raymond was whistling his favorite old song, "Le Temps des cerises" ("The Time of Cherries"). Thomas felt like he was reliving a morning from his childhood, with him in the kitchen of his family's apartment and his father making breakfast.

"Do you still like your bread just lightly toasted? I'm pretending I can actually touch things. Pretending is fun sometimes. It's like being alive again for a minute, you know? You always used to sit at the table, where you would open your notebook and pretend too. You would act as if you were reading, but in reality, you were watching me. I could feel your eyes on my shoulder blades, and I enjoyed your silence. I would put the plate down in front of you, with the jam on the side, because that's the way you liked it. You were already very particular about your food. I would unfold my newspaper, and then it was my turn to watch you, discreetly, as you ate. You would gulp down your milk and look me right in the eyes. Then you would take your plate to the sink, kiss my forehead without a word, and head to the stairwell to wait for me. Every time I walked you to school—"

"I would ask you what surgeries you had lined up for the day. Once, you tried to convince me that you were operating on a man born with two heads, and you had no idea how to choose which one to cut off. That story scared me to death."

Raymond burst into laughter. "It wasn't a total lie. Some other doctors, English ones, had just managed to separate twins conjoined by their occipital lobes. That's where I got the idea. A crazy but rather funny one, I thought. So, have you made your decision?"

Thomas opened the refrigerator and pulled out a bag of sliced bread. He put two pieces on a plate alongside a spoonful of jam, grabbed his laptop, and sat down at the table. As he ate, he typed away at the computer, his father watching in fascination.

"You type so fast! I can't believe I used to type my reports with two fingers. It took forever!"

"I'm a pianist. Quick fingers are part of the gig."

"Who are you writing to, if I may ask?" asked Raymond.

"Okayabitz."

"A foreign friend?"

"An online travel agency. Don't get too excited. I'm just seeing if what you're asking is even possible, and how much it would cost. When's the funeral?"

"In three days."

"I'm playing in Warsaw next Saturday, and there's no way I can cancel at the last minute. If we were to leave tomorrow," Thomas mused out loud, clicking through the flight options, "with the nine-hour time difference, we'd arrive the same day. That would give me over twenty-four hours to come up with a plan. Do you know where the funeral will be?"

"In a crematorium. Where else would a cremation take place?"

"Fantastic. Who doesn't dream of visiting San Francisco and its famous crematoriums? And on Wednesday . . . no, I'm not even going to think about what I would have to do on Wednesday. Then a flight back to Paris on Thursday, arriving Friday morning. And off to Warsaw on Saturday morning."

"Is it very expensive?"

"It's certainly not cheap."

"But you can afford it?"

"A thousand euros, right next to the bathroom."

"Flying *coach*?"

The look Thomas gave Raymond was answer enough.

"Plus, we have to find somewhere to stay—at least, *I* do."

"Oh, right. I didn't think of that."

"I did." Thomas resumed his rapid typing.

"Who are you writing to now?"

"I'm on another website, looking for a room to rent in somebody's apartment. Here's an affordable one. Sixty dollars a night on the ground floor of a small Victorian on Green Street. They even speak French. Let's just hope the crematorium isn't on the other side of town."

Thomas went and grabbed his wallet from the pocket of his jacket, which was hanging off the back of a chair.

"What are you doing?" Raymond asked.

"Good question! The answer, apparently, is that I'm getting ready to take a little trip with my dad while trying not to think about the fact that he's been dead for five years."

"Can I ask one more favor?"

"Why not? What's one more at this point?"

"Tell me how I look."

"You look like yourself. I rarely saw you wear anything other than a straight-cut blazer, cuffed tweed pants, and freshly shined loafers, just like the ones you're wearing now."

"I wasn't asking for a description. I'm asking, Is it elegant?"

"You've always looked elegant, even on the weekends. It impressed me very much when I was a kid."

"That was the goal," his father replied proudly. "I'm just asking because, well, if all goes to plan, Camille and I will be together again. And I want to make sure I look my best. It's hard to keep up with style trends when you're dead, you know."

Suddenly, Thomas realized something shocking. His father appeared significantly younger than he had the day he died. He in fact looked like he had in his fifties, like he did in the picture Thomas always carried with him—a photograph of the two of them together, taken on vacation one summer.

"Your hair is a little bit messy, but it adds a nice rebel edge to your look."

"Did you buy the plane tickets?" his father asked, impatient.

"I bought mine."

"Of course! No need for the senior citizen discount now! I travel for free. My condition includes a few perks, don't you think? When do we leave?"

"Tomorrow morning. Now, I'm going to pack and take advantage of my last free day."

"Don't forget you have to pick up my urn from your mother's house."

"And just how am I supposed to explain why I'm borrowing your ashes?"

"Good question. We need a plan. Do you still have a key to her place?"

Jeanne was surprised to see Thomas again so soon.

"Aren't you supposed to be playing in Vienna tonight?" she asked as she opened the door.

"No. No more concerts until Saturday, in Warsaw."

"Vienna, Warsaw—it's hard to keep track of all your dates and venues. I used to follow it all very closely, but I don't have the time anymore."

"I didn't realize you were so busy," Thomas said.

"Sweetheart, when you reach a certain age, time becomes unpredictable. It flies when you're having fun and drags on when you're bored. Since no one needs me anymore, I decided to simply have as much fun as possible for as long as possible."

"You know I still need you," Thomas said, giving her a hug.

"Stop, you're tickling me," she said with a laugh. "And you're going to mess up my hair. I'm going out tonight."

"Again?"

"And tomorrow too."

"Are you seeing someone?"

"What do you mean 'seeing someone'? I see lots of people."

"Fine, don't tell me."

"So, what brings you here?"

"Can't a son come see his mother without a reason?"

"It's not to smoke one of my special cigarettes, is it?"

"No, I'll leave those to you."

"Hmm, what could it be then?" His mother glanced over to her two armchairs. She chose the one on the left and invited him to sit down in the other.

"You look worn out. Would you like me to make you something to eat?"

Thomas shook his head.

"Is it a broken heart?"

"No, I don't have even one woman on my radar . . ."

"Thomas, you look exactly like your father, but other than that, you're nothing like him. I don't understand why you're still single."

"Why are you so obsessed with me settling down?"

"Because I'd like to be a grandmother."

"There's plenty of time for that."

"Maybe for *you*."

"Let's not spend the whole day sitting here chatting about baby clothes," his father stage-whispered from the couch.

"Could you please just let me do things at my own speed!"

"There's no need to speak to me in that tone," his mother said.

Thomas apologized. Jeanne looked confused by the angry glance he shot at the couch.

"Back in the day, whenever you were going through a breakup or were falling in love, you would call me, and we'd spend whole nights talking about it. I miss that a lot."

"Ever since things ended with Sophie, my life has been a blur, my work taking me from city to city. Not exactly ideal conditions for—"

"And now we get the complete history of your personal life?" Raymond sighed. "Did you love this Sophie or not?"

"Yes. Well . . . I don't know."

"What don't you know?" asked his mother.

"If I really loved Sophie."

"In that case, you're better off without her," his parents both said, practically in unison.

"A smile at last!" rejoiced Jeanne. "I was beginning to think this was a funeral."

"You have no idea!" Thomas blurted out without thinking.

"Really? Who died?" his mother asked, her curiosity obviously piqued.

"No one in particular. I mean, I imagine someone somewhere has died. Never mind. Let's change the subject."

"You're acting very strange these days."

"So I've been told."

"Why are you walking around with that old shopping bag?"

"I was going to buy groceries."

"This is all a waste of time!" Raymond cut in. "Tell your mother you're hungry. While she's in the kitchen, you can steal the urn. We can't spend all day here."

"Would you please make me a sandwich?" asked Thomas.

"Of course, sweetheart. That's what mothers are for. I'll be back in a minute."

"To the office, hurry!" Raymond exclaimed.

Thomas obeyed his father. To be safe, he peeked his head into the hallway before going in, to make sure his mother wasn't hanging around nearby. He could hear her humming in the kitchen.

"Operation Office!" his father announced, as if they were high-ranking military officials.

"Operation Ridiculous, if you ask me," grumbled Thomas.

Raymond's former office hadn't changed a bit. It was a large, inviting room with French doors that opened onto a wide balcony. The walls—covered in expensive beige wallpaper—perfectly complemented the oak floor. Massive bookcases stood on either side of a fireplace that hadn't heated the room in quite some time.

"Look on the top shelf," his father suggested. "Probably near the window."

Thomas stood on his tiptoes and reached up, feeling around behind the books for the urn.

Jeanne assembled a quick sandwich with cold cuts from the fridge. When she came back to the living room, carrying the tray, she was surprised to see it empty. The noise in the next room led her to leave the tray on the coffee table and quietly pad into the office.

She was even more intrigued when she found Thomas perched on his tiptoes.

"Are you looking for a particular book?" she asked.

Thomas jumped and turned around.

"Where are Dad's ashes?" he asked abruptly.

"That's one way to do it," muttered his father.

"I used them to test my new bagless vacuum. Oh, don't look at me like that, I was joking! I'm sure they're where they've always been, though I've never checked. Still, I doubt your father's escaped. Funny, he never spent this much time at home when he was alive."

"Do you ever miss him?"

"Would you mind saving this kind of conversation for another day?" Raymond protested. "One when I'm not around, for example . . ."

"Well, then, go away!" whispered Thomas.

"Excuse me?" his mother replied. "You are really acting very strange today. And by the way, you're looking in the wrong place. Your father is on the other side of the fireplace, on the top shelf, behind *Madame Bovary*. It was my little act of revenge. Here, use the armchair to climb up. I don't feel like going back to the kitchen for the step stool."

Raymond buttoned his jacket and disappeared, clearly troubled.

Thomas pushed an armchair—the one in which his father's ghost had first appeared to him—over to the bookcase. There, he finally found what he was looking for. Reaching behind *A Sentimental Education*, which was just as dusty as the neighboring copy of *Madame Bovary*, he finally got his hands on the urn.

"There's a small wooden box next to it," his mother said. "Take that while you're at it. If you feel like diving into your father's history, or worshiping his memory, its contents will no doubt tell you more about him than his ashes will."

"Can I take his urn with me?" asked Thomas.

"You may as well, given that you were planning to hide it in your shopping bag anyway. Remind me: How old are you, again?"

Thomas had the uncomfortable feeling that he was eight years old again, and had just been caught with his hand in the cookie jar.

"Come on, let's go back to the living room," she said. "This office depresses me. I never stay long."

Obviously intuiting that Thomas didn't want to stay any longer, his mother led him to the kitchen, where she wrapped the urn in newspaper and placed it in the shopping bag, smiling the whole time.

"It's all yours. He asked the two of us to keep the urn and its contents, but he never said which of us was ultimately responsible for them. It's your turn now, and good riddance from me. It will do you good to reconnect with him. The two of you grew apart toward the end of his life. What? Why are you looking at me like that? What did I say this time?"

"Sometimes I can't decide whether you or Dad was the crazier one."

"Funny. Have you seen what you look like carrying that thing? Plus, why do you think the two of us got married in the first place? If your father hadn't been at least a little nuts, you wouldn't exist, my darling. Now, go on, get out of here. Have a little chat with him. I have to get ready."

7

Thomas went straight home. His father hadn't spoken a word the whole way. When they got inside, Thomas put the urn down on the table.

"Are you going to sulk all day?" he asked, breaking the long silence.

"Wrapped up in newspaper at the bottom of an old shopping bag! Have you no shame? What am I, the special of the day?"

"You're overreacting, if you ask me."

Thomas went to pack. He slipped his passport into his suitcase but held on to his toiletries bag for a moment, a thoughtful expression on his face.

"You never know," he finally muttered, grabbing his cologne.

He then unwrapped the urn, opened the lid, and spritzed in some fragrance.

"What in the world are you doing? Have you lost your mind?" his father objected, jumping to his feet.

"When was the last time you flew?"

"I don't know. What difference does it make?"

"Trust me. You'll thank me for this. Anyway, it's not like you can stop me."

"Thomas, if I reek of patchouli when I'm reunited with Camille, I will never forgive you."

"Don't worry, the scent is vetiver. Now, I'm going out for dinner. Alone!"

"Harsh words. But you should know that this little adventure we're about to embark on could make one of your dreams come true too."

"Given the circumstances and what you're asking me to do, I can't for the life of me imagine what dream that would be."

"Haven't you always dreamed of performing at Carnegie Hall? Why don't you audition during this trip?"

"Because Carnegie Hall is in New York, not California."

Thomas saw no point in continuing the discussion. He grabbed his jacket and left, hurrying down the stairs two at a time.

The springtime scent of renewal wafted through the streets of Paris. The chestnut trees were in full bloom, and Thomas looked up to admire the red and pink petals peeking out from between the leaves.

As he walked, he decided to cross a square that was overrun with weeds and trash. It always shocked him to see how dirty the most beautiful city in the world could become. He'd strolled the streets of Amsterdam, Madrid, London, Prague, Vienna, Budapest, and Stockholm, and not a single one of them could compare to Paris's trash. Only Rome had been littered with as much garbage. He'd mentioned this to Sophie one day, and she'd accused him of acting like an old man. Thomas didn't understand what clean streets had to do with age. What she could have meant was just one of her many mysteries. The memory of their argument reminded him of the many messages his friend Serge—who was always breaking up and getting back together with his girlfriend—had sent recently. Thomas called him now to invite him to dinner at a bistro. No doubt the evening wouldn't be particularly cheery, but listening to a friend's misery wouldn't be all that bad. Serge's misfortunes might help him to see that his life wasn't so terrible after all, and his heartaches would no doubt remind Thomas that the single life has its advantages.

They met at L'Ami Jean, Thomas's favorite restaurant in Paris. Serge complained at first about the shared, cafeteria-style table, which wasn't ideal for serious discussions, but Thomas reassured him. The people to their right were speaking Japanese, and the diners to the left were most likely Australian, given their accent.

Thomas displayed a remarkable stoicism throughout the meal. If his neighbors had understood everything he was enduring in listening to Serge, they would have agreed. Fortunately, Thomas had a gift for daydreaming. He'd first discovered this talent while at school. No bored math student had ever shown a greater ability to flee the classroom with their mind. And this first gift had led to a second: Ever since he was very young, Thomas had imagined melodies so vividly it was as if he were hearing them in a concert hall. They echoed through his head as if by magic, beckoning him to imaginary journeys. While Serge listed the countless ways his girlfriend had displayed a lack of care for him, Thomas let himself be carried away by Schubert's impromptus. First, the one in C minor transported him to an evening in Stockholm made memorable because the Swedes are such wonderful listeners. Next, Impromptu No. 2 evoked a fall afternoon in Paris and kisses with a law student. What had her name been again?

"Are you even listening to me?" asked Serge.

"Of course," Thomas assured him as Impromptu No. 3 brought his father to mind. Thomas had performed the piece the day after Raymond's death, without anyone in the audience knowing that his black tie and tails doubled as mourning attire.

He shouldn't have left his father alone tonight; he was wasting such a rare, impossible opportunity. Why, since his father had appeared, hadn't he tried to have a real conversation with him? He regretted all the silences there had been between them, all the things left unsaid. And yet here he was, with Serge.

"Don't look so sad," Serge continued. "Even if she leaves me, life goes on, right?"

"Yes and no," said Thomas. Impromptu No. 4 arrived in time to rescue him, whisking him off to Tuscany, just before his twentieth birthday. Her name had been Fabiola, and she'd had magnificent breasts, her skin as soft and inviting as fine linen. Her hands were so gentle. Whatever had happened to her?

"Do you think I should make the first move?" asked Serge.

"Whatever happened to her?" Thomas said, out loud this time.

"Since yesterday? That's a strange question."

"Please stop. I've had enough of people calling me 'strange' for one day."

"What are you talking about?"

"Nothing," Thomas said. "Go on."

"So, should I call her or not?"

At that moment, the Trio for Piano in E Major popped into his head—a delightful melody. One morning at the conservatory, when their teacher had been late, he and some friends had messed around, playing it jazz-style. They'd all stopped laughing instantly when their teacher, a vain conductor, had come in shouting that Schubert was rolling in his grave. Thomas was punished for snapping back that they were simply providing an opportunity for the composer to roll back into his original position, after all the writhing he'd surely done while listening to the teacher conduct Symphony No. 3.

"Call her," Thomas replied, still amused by his memory.

"Would you mind telling me what's so funny?"

"I'm just happy to be having dinner with you."

"I suppose you're right. What's the worst thing that can happen if I make the first move?"

"That you make the second move as well and then call me in a month to tell me you're unhappy. I'm sorry, but we're going to have to skip dessert. I really need to get home. I'm leaving at the crack of dawn tomorrow."

"Where are you off to?"

"San Francisco."

"Good for you!" exclaimed Serge. "You've been dreaming of playing on an American stage for forever."

"It's not for a concert." Thomas gestured to the waiter to bring the check.

"I see. What's her name, then?"

"You're not even close. I'm actually taking my father on a trip," Thomas continued, hunting for his credit card.

Serge watched him, a strange look on his face.

"That was a metaphor," Thomas corrected himself. "Don't look at me as if I've lost my mind. If you must know, I'm going on a kind of pilgrimage."

"I don't need to know. Shall we split the check?"

"No, I'll let you get it this time. My plane ticket cleaned me out, but I promise it's on me next time. And now, I really have to go. He's waiting for me."

Thomas waved goodbye and ran out to the street to catch a taxi, which shortly dropped him in front of his building. He ran up the stairs and found his apartment empty. Disappointed, he called to his father. He opened the door to the closet in the foolish hope that his father would be hiding there, then went into the bathroom and leaned out the window to get a good look at the rooftops.

"Maybe you're out. If you can hear me, don't stay out too late. The alarm is set for dawn. It's going to be a long trip."

Suddenly, Thomas felt very alone. He wondered, as he headed to bed, if perhaps he was losing his mind after all.

Thomas woke up from a restless sleep at the first ray of light. He rubbed his head as he opened his eyes and called out to his father, but all he could hear was a city employee whistling as he swept the sidewalk in front of the building.

If his suitcase weren't sitting right there on the dresser, Thomas would have assumed he was simply emerging from a very strange dream.

"What game are you playing, Dad? Or are you simply sulking again? If you want to miss the plane, just tell me. It'll be easier that way," he called out.

When he received no reply, he shrugged and made his way to the shower. Then he got dressed, made coffee, and paced around the apartment.

"What joke are you trying to pull on me?"

Thomas began to wonder about his mental health once more. With a frown, he studied the urn sticking out of his bag.

"Have you abandoned me again? Do you want me to go on this trip alone?" he asked, a little hopelessly. "Fine. Have it your way." He carried his suitcase outside and closed his front door. "I'll see to your last wishes and then we'll be even."

A taxi was parked outside, waiting for him. On the drive to the airport, Thomas turned around at least ten times to watch Paris fade into the distance through the back window.

At the check-in counter, the airline employee asked if he was traveling alone and Thomas answered, "Mostly."

He stopped at a magazine shop and bought a copy of the monthly music magazine *Diapason* (that is, "tuning fork"), which he then flipped through as he enjoyed a macaron from the Ladurée counter—Ladurée macarons were one of his favorite treats.

When he'd finally worked up the courage, Thomas walked toward the security checkpoint. A dark mass appeared on the screen, and the agent frowned and confiscated his bag for a more detailed inspection.

"What is this?" asked the young security agent as she took hold of the urn.

"A jar of incense," Thomas said. "I'm a concert pianist, and it helps to calm my nerves."

"You must be really anxious to need this much. May I?" she asked as she opened the lid.

Thomas nodded and blinked in agreement. She bent closer and sniffed the contents. "It smells nice," she said as she closed it.

She checked the urn for traces of explosives, then finally returned it to Thomas. He put it back in his bag, told the woman goodbye, and left. His anxiety grew as he looked around the gate area.

"I feel like a lost child in a crowd, desperately searching for his parents," he mumbled. "This is all so ridiculous."

Thomas briefly considered turning around and going home but then decided it would be silly to miss out on visiting San Francisco, since he'd already paid for his flight and come all the way to the airport. He hurried down the gangway and into the airplane cabin, where he stored his bag in the overhead bin.

His neighbor had already claimed the armrest between them and had unfolded her newspaper, taking up the entirety of her space and some of Thomas's as well.

He glanced at the empty seat across the aisle, hoping he would be able to move to it once boarding was complete.

As soon as the head flight attendant announced that the doors were closing, his father appeared in the seat, a huge grin on his face.

"Admit it! You missed me a little."

"You think this is funny? Is this some kind of game to you?"

"Do you really think it's that easy to reincarnate? I was there in the room with you, but for some reason, you couldn't see me. I guess it was some kind of glitch. Your cologne trick was brilliant, by the way."

"A glitch?"

"A wonderfully American word, isn't it?"

"You want to hear about a glitch? I was about to turn my back on this whole thing. How's that for a glitch?"

"Oh, I heard you grumbling, but you wouldn't have given up. What did you mean when you said we'd be even? Am I to understand that you've finally decided that the upbringing I gave you was good enough after all?"

Thomas's neighbor folded up her paper with a compassionate smile. She reassured him that he had nothing to worry about since air travel was the safest means of transportation. In an apparent attempt to distract him, she asked him what he did for a living.

"I'm a pianist," he replied.

"They have excellent musical channels on board. Nothing better to help you relax," she said as she put on her headphones.

Thomas glared at his father, who seemed to be enjoying the situation.

"By the way, what an evening last night! Your friend Serge is terribly boring. I think his girlfriend had the right idea—I would have left him once and for all a long time ago."

Thomas decided to use his neighbor's idea to block out his father. He grabbed his headphones and closed his eyes as the plane took off.

As Thomas slept, his father watched over him silently. When the flight attendants brought the meal, he leaned in toward his son.

"I thought you wanted to make up for lost time."

"I don't think this is the best place for a chat—that is, unless you want to see me put in a straitjacket."

"Fair enough. But I can still talk."

"My God, for someone who was so reserved in life, you've certainly become chatty in death!"

"Would you stop invoking God for every little thing? I'm not exactly sure how high up the information about my leave went . . . And if I didn't talk much back then, well, maybe it was because you never asked me any questions."

Thomas glanced at his neighbor, who was watching him suspiciously.

"If you're that worried about what that woman thinks of you, why don't you write down what you want to say to me."

Thomas found the idea ridiculous. "We've waited thirty-five years to get all this off our chests. We can wait a little longer, until we get off this plane."

"What exactly do you need to get off your chest? You don't see me holding a grudge."

"That's not what I meant."

"But it's what you said. Are you going to act like an immature child and say I didn't care about you enough? Fine, let's get on with it, then. But I get to go first, since I'm older. So, tell me, what was my favorite movie, my favorite song? Which poem moved me the most in life? Here we are: checkmate in a single move. You have no idea, do you? Admit it, you were going to try to trap me with exactly that sort of question."

"So, being dead gives you the power to read my mind?"

"Being your father gave me that power a long time ago."

"*Bread and Chocolate*, 'Singin' in the Rain,' which you sang in the shower and in the car on your way home, and Rimbaud's 'The Sleeper in the Valley.' I think you've just lost your king."

Raymond looked steadily at his son.

"I would take you to spend Saturday afternoons at the Jardin d'Acclimatation amusement park, and as soon as we'd get home, you'd ask for your mother and throw yourself into her arms. I went to all your soccer matches, but you played for her. I would give you your bath or read your stories, but you still wanted her to put you to bed. Whenever I would come into your room in the morning, you were always disappointed she wasn't the one who'd come to wake you up."

"Mom took care of me all the time—not just on Saturday afternoons. She took me to school and picked me up every day. And whenever we got home, I always asked her what time you would be back; it's just that you weren't there to hear it. Mom asked me about my day and didn't just keep reading the newspaper while I talked. She was gentle with me. She was patient."

"You see? The question was never whether I spent enough time with you. I simply wasn't raised to give you all those things. Blame masculine stoicism—I couldn't even hug you for more than a few seconds without getting uncomfortable. My whole life I've struggled with affection. I was the surgeon people felt emotionally distant from, and yet, even when I was operating, I did it with love. I knew men who boasted about all the hearts they'd broken. I tried to put hearts back together."

"Yes, spleens, livers, appendixes, and probably a whole lot of other organs too. I don't need the details."

"That woman is so annoying, giving us those strange looks. Tell her you're schizophrenic so she'll leave us alone!"

"I'm not sure she'd find that reassuring at thirty thousand feet."

"Be quiet for a minute," whispered Raymond. "Something's going on up front."

"How can you tell? We're in the back row."

"I can feel it. There's agitation in the air. You don't hear anything?"

"Death seems to be treating you well. You do remember that your hearing wasn't the best those last few years, right?"

"Selective hearing, son. One of the rare privileges of old age is only hearing what interests you and pretending you missed the rest."

"You were faking it?"

"Let's just say I sorted useful information from superfluous chatter. Plus, being hard of hearing spares you from quite a few chores. What's the point of asking someone who can't hear to take out the trash?"

The pilot's voice came on over the intercom. A passenger in first class needed medical attention. If there was a doctor on board, he or she should alert a member of the crew.

"What did I tell you!" Raymond exclaimed.

"That you were a rather cold fish."

"Raise your hand," Raymond ordered.

"Why on earth would I do that?"

"Have you seen anyone else volunteer?"

"No, but I'm not a doctor."

"I am, though. Flag down that flight attendant. You are so stubborn sometimes. Think of the passenger who needs help, for goodness' sake!"

Suddenly, Thomas felt his hand begin to jerk around. Unable to control it, he watched as it waved in the air overhead.

"Are you doing that?" he asked, stunned.

"No, it's your conscience, genius."

His neighbor gave him a look filled with both sympathy and surprise.

"You must have misheard. Probably due to your anxiety," she offered, with a fake laugh. "They need a doctor, not a pianist."

"I know," Thomas sighed.

"So, why are you raising your hand?"

"Ah, see, that I do not know," he said with a shrug.

"Well, put it down, then!"

"I can't, it's beyond my control."

"But there's no point in serenading that poor sick man," she argued.

"I doubt there's a piano on board. And to be honest, serenades get on everyone's nerves after a while, not just sick people's."

"What are you playing at?"

"It depends on the evening. Brahms, Mozart, Bruch . . ."

"Are you messing with me?"

"I promise, I'm not," Thomas exclaimed as sincerely as possible. "Let go of my hand, Dad. You're going to get me in trouble!"

The woman stared at him, dumbfounded.

"Oh, I wasn't talking to you," he apologized.

She leaned over to look in the direction of the seemingly empty seat where Raymond—visible only to Thomas—was enjoying every second of the show.

"Are you on something?" she asked.

"Just a plane, same as you."

A flight attendant came over, putting an end to the doomed conversation. She thanked Thomas for volunteering, explained that a passenger had passed out, and asked him to follow her.

His seatmate couldn't believe her eyes as he stood up. "But he's a pianist!" she protested.

Her protest fell on deaf ears. Thomas was already halfway up the aisle. The stage fright he felt before a performance was nothing compared to what he felt as he reached the first rows of the plane.

A man in his fifties was lying unconscious on the galley floor, where the crew had carried him to give him some room.

"We need more space," Raymond exclaimed. "That is, your patient needs it. Ask the two male flight attendants to go take care of the other passengers, so there's more room. Keep only the woman here with you. Ask her what happened before he passed out," he ordered.

"It would be better if there were fewer people around," Thomas suggested shyly. "But could you stay and explain what happened?" he asked the woman.

The two male flight attendants left. The woman clearly felt flattered to have been chosen to help the young doctor.

"He asked me for something to drink. When I brought him a glass of water, he seemed agitated and was sweating heavily. At first, I thought he was having a panic attack because of the turbulence. He wasn't making sense and started acting aggressively. He kept asking for his bag and was wheezing as if he couldn't breathe. Then his face went white and he fainted. Do you think it's a heart attack?"

"Maybe, but I suspect something else," Thomas heard himself say, as if his father had possessed him. Then he watched as he took the man's pulse and declared that it was slow but steady.

"Take his hand and tell me if it's cold," said his father. "I can't do that part."

Thomas grabbed the man's hand awkwardly, as if he were shaking it, surprising the flight attendant.

"Cold," he mumbled.

"All right, now lean in toward his mouth and tell me if it smells like apples."

"Are you kidding me? This isn't *House*," groaned Thomas, citing the medical TV show. The flight attendant raised her eyebrow.

"Do as I tell you!"

"His breath doesn't smell like apples," Thomas said, straightening up as the flight attendant stared.

"So, he's not in ketoacidosis," Raymond concluded. "Push hard on one of his cheeks, at the place where the jawbones meet. Don't ask me why."

Thomas did as he was told, and the man moaned.

"Now we know he's just unconscious, not in a coma," explained the surgeon. Raymond ordered his son to roll up the man's sleeves and look for needle marks.

"There's a big one," Thomas said in a confident tone. And once again he found himself speaking without intending to: "Didn't you say he'd asked for his bag?"

"Yes," the flight attendant replied cautiously.

"Bring it here."

She hesitated, then complied.

"Are you sure you know what you're doing?" she asked, handing over the man's luggage.

"I sure hope so." Thomas sighed.

His father scowled. "Keep your snide remarks to yourself and go through his bag. You'll most likely find a long, rectangular, orange plastic case containing glucagon. We'll need that."

Thomas found the kit just as his father had predicted. He opened it and discovered a syringe filled with a solution and a bottle containing a powder.

"Now, do exactly as I say. It's easy, you'll see. First, take the seal off the bottle, then plunge the needle through the plastic lid and push down on the plunger to empty the solution into the powder. Just like that, perfect. Now mix it all up. And now suck the mixture back up into the syringe. I'm impressed, you've done really well."

"And now?" Thomas asked worriedly.

"Lift up the front of his shirt. Use your left hand to pinch some flesh between your thumb and your forefinger, to create a fold. Hold the syringe like a dart, making sure not to touch the plunger."

"There's no way I can give this guy a shot," Thomas said under his breath.

"Of course you can, you're perfectly capable."

"No," he said, his hands shaking.

"Are you all right?" asked the flight attendant.

Thomas was holding the syringe just a few inches from the man's stomach when his seatmate burst in behind them.

"This man is not a doctor! He told me so himself!" she protested vehemently.

Her expression filling with doubt, the flight attendant appeared about to intervene when Thomas stuck the needle into the man's skin and emptied the syringe. Everyone was silent for a moment. The flight attendant stared at Thomas, who kept his eyes glued on the passenger. Thomas's angry neighbor held her breath, and Raymond made sounds of rejoicing.

The man came to and asked where he was. Thomas's seatmate threw up her hands and left, swearing that she wasn't crazy—unlike *some* people on this plane.

Thomas helped the flight attendant take the passenger back to his seat, reciting his father's instructions word for word. "Give him something sweet to drink. And you, sir, check your blood sugar regularly until we land."

"Thank you, doctor," the flight attendant and the passenger replied practically in unison, to Raymond's delight.

The flight attendant said she wished she could invite Thomas to finish the trip in first class, but the cabin was full.

"Don't worry, it was no trouble," he assured her.

He went back to his seat and leaned over toward his neighbor, who was still all worked up. "There's no rule that says I can't be a doctor *and* a pianist," he said.

"Looks like your dear old dad still has what it takes," Raymond said. "You did good, kid."

"I guess so, but what if he hadn't woken up? I would have ended up in handcuffs for risking a man's life!"

"Is he dead, or is he feeling better? You should be proud of yourself for taking such a big risk to help save someone. Are you going to hold *this* against me now?" Raymond asked with a hint of irony in his voice.

Thomas thought for a moment, then turned to his father and asked, "What exactly happened while I was helping that man?"

"While *we* were helping him! I seem to remember giving you some assistance."

"That's exactly what I mean. Was it just a feeling I got, or were you actually talking through me?"

"A feeling, I guess. I wouldn't have dared."

"That's strange. I said things that don't make sense to me and used words I don't know. It was as if I was possessed."

"So what? The important thing is what you did, not what you said."

"Don't ever do that again. It was a terrible feeling. It was like you existed *within me.*"

"Every parent's dream! Living on in their children's hearts," Raymond replied in a joking tone. "Don't make a big thing out of it. Your mother used to speak for you all the time when you were young. I'd ask you a question and she would answer."

"Were you always this jealous of her?"

"I have no idea what you're talking about. Now, get some rest. We have a lot of work ahead of us."

The plane flew over San Francisco Bay. As it turned left, Thomas could see the bright-red outline of the Golden Gate Bridge hovering over the water.

Thomas felt better as he left the plane. The man in first class had gotten off first. The flight attendant thanked Thomas warmly at the door.

Thomas returned her smile and made his way up the gangway.

"Why don't you ask for her number? She must be here for at least two days before she returns to Paris. You could invite her to dinner tomorrow night."

"And do what? Lie to her by continuing to pretend that I'm a doctor? You act as if I had nothing else planned for this trip."

"I have your best interests at heart. It seems I left you much too soon. I still had so much to teach you."

"Mom said something along the same lines recently."

"Really? When exactly did she say that?"

"Maybe you should keep quiet while I go through immigration," said Thomas as he got in the line that seemed to have no end.

"Why don't you come right out and ask me to shut up, then."

"I just did."

Thomas watched nervously as the immigration officer inspected his passport. If this man asked him to open his bag, Thomas felt sure he would do more than sniff the contents of the urn. When the officer asked why he was in the United States, Thomas said it was for a funeral. The man didn't have any more questions after that, and just an hour after landing, Thomas found himself sitting in a taxi on his way to the city.

As the Transamerica Pyramid came into view in the distance, Raymond seemed troubled. "She's here," he whispered, "I can feel it. I haven't been this close to her in more than twenty years. It's quite moving, isn't it?"

Thomas looked at his father. Seeing him so shaken made him feel something too.

"Yes. I guess we aren't far now. I'll do everything I can, I promise."

"I know, son," his father said, and he patted Thomas's leg in the same way he had so many times before.

8

The taxi stopped in front of a typical Pacific Heights Victorian on Green Street. Thomas paid the driver, grabbed his bag, and rang the doorbell.

A woman in her forties, radiant and with a natural look, opened the door.

"Hi, I'm Thomas," he said, holding out his hand.

"Lauren Kline. I was afraid your flight would be late. I have to be at the hospital in an hour, so I really need to go. Follow me and I'll give you a quick tour."

"Are you a doctor, then?" Thomas asked as he stepped inside.

"Yes, why?"

"No reason."

"Do you have some sort of health problem?" Lauren asked with concern as she made her way down the stairs to the rental.

"No, everything's fine in the health department."

"Glad to hear it. Here we are." She opened the door to the apartment. "The bedroom is to the right, and the bathroom and living room are on the left, plus a kitchenette."

Thomas studied the room. The wood floor was made of wide boards. There was a couch covered with a blanket, an old coffee table, four wicker chairs, and a colorful rug. The decor was a little mismatched, but it created a cheerful atmosphere. The four windows—two looked out onto the street, two onto the flower-filled yard—filled the space with light.

"We live just upstairs," his host explained, "but you won't hear us. My husband is in Carmel today and won't be home until early evening. And I'll be back very late. Doctors' hours aren't the best."

"I know," Thomas replied.

"Is your wife a doctor?"

"No, my father was a surgeon."

"Has he retired? What was his specialty?"

"Cardiothoracic. He lived for the operating table, but he's no longer with us."

"I'm sorry. What brings you to San Francisco? You're only staying three nights, right?"

Thomas hesitated, then confessed he'd crossed the Atlantic to attend a funeral.

"Someone close to you? Obviously, otherwise you wouldn't have traveled so far."

"Actually, I barely knew her. She was my father's mistress."

Lauren offered a wry smile.

"We went to France three years ago. My husband's best friend lives in Paris, and we went to visit him."

"Did you like it there?"

"So much. Parisians say exactly what they think. It's irresistible."

"You must not have stayed very long, then. Look, I don't want to keep you. Your home is lovely. It'll be perfect, don't worry about a thing."

"If you need anything, Arthur will be home this evening. He'll be delighted to meet you."

Lauren warned him not to worry if he heard something like the sound of gunshots coming from the garage—starting her old car was a little tricky. Then she was off.

Moments later, he heard the engine backfire. He looked out the window to see a green Triumph zooming down Green Street.

"What a lead foot!" Raymond exclaimed. "I like her, she's got character."

"The surgeon or the car?" asked Thomas.

"By the way, thank you for singing my praises to her in that elegant way you have. Would you like to go for a walk, or would you rather stay here and make more little jokes?"

Thomas opened the door to the bedroom. There was an old dresser stacked high with books, a wing chair next to the window, a jute rug, a large bed covered with a quilt, and two birch nightstands. The overall effect was charming.

"Which side do you want?" Raymond joked.

Thomas looked at his watch instead of answering. He was desperate to go to sleep, but he knew he had to stay awake to keep the jet lag at bay.

He took a shower, changed clothes, and then went for a walk on the neighborhood's main street. A sign of the times, an old movie theater on Union Street that still featured its historic facade was now home to a gym. Thomas strolled in and out of several shops, then stepped into an art gallery that had the works of local artists on display.

Raymond stopped in front of a small pastel of a beach in the Presidio.

"This one's not half bad," he said. "Great lines in India ink and delicate colors. If you're in the market for a gift for your mother, this would be perfect without breaking the bank."

Thomas looked straight at his father. "You have to stop that."

"What am I doing wrong now?"

"Speaking through me, reading my thoughts. This," he said, pointing to his forehead, "is a line I forbid you to cross!"

"You're being totally paranoid. Who do you think I am, anyway? An angel with supernatural gifts? That's flattering, thanks, but you've got it all wrong. I'm just your father."

"What about that little game you played on the plane? You think that's normal?"

"I loaned you my voice, true, but I have no idea how it works. The urgency of the situation must have flipped some switch in me. I wouldn't have any idea how to do it again. As for the painting, well, it's a gorgeous day outside, and instead of enjoying it, you're wandering around a bunch of shops, so I figured you must be looking for something to buy. And since you're single, I knew it had to be for your mother. It doesn't take a ghost to figure that out. So, now that my name's been cleared, are you going to buy it or not?"

Thomas exited the store with the painting. He walked a few paces down the street and sat at a table on the terrace at Perry's, where he ordered a beer.

"Your mother will love it," Raymond said, glancing at the gift bag at Thomas's feet. "That said, it also would have been a perfect gift for a sweetheart, if you had one . . ."

"That's a bit of a dated term."

"No, it's charming. What on earth do you like so much about being single? It's boring!"

"I'm not sure you're the best person to give me this lecture. Has it truly never occurred to you that you and Mom's divorce may have given me commitment issues?"

"Oh, don't play the victim. The reason you're so afraid of commitment is because you put your career first, your music, your trips . . . It's all rather selfish. Order something to eat; you shouldn't go to bed hungry."

"Hmm . . ."

"Your 'hmms' are starting to get on my nerves."

"What about you? Do you sleep at night since you've died?" Thomas asked.

"Let me put it this way: Day and night don't mean much to me anymore, but the idea of eternal rest is a scam."

"I thought you weren't allowed to tell me anything about it."

"I didn't tell you anything. You drew your own conclusions about whether I sleep or not, didn't you? They can't hold a simple conversation with my son against me. And by the way, if I do slip up, please keep it to yourself."

"Who could I ever tell this to without sounding like a nut job?"

"Don't say that. Someday, you'll meet someone, and the two of you will write a beautiful story together, you'll see. And you'll be able to tell her everything, even your craziest thoughts."

"Could you do that with Camille?"

"I did it with your mother."

Raymond looked at the menu and suggested a hamburger. "When traveling, it's always best to opt for local cuisine," he added.

Thomas ordered a salad.

"I've figured out what your problem is. You don't laugh enough, son."

"I know what you're going to say next: 'You only live once.'"

"No, that's also a load of nonsense. The truth is that you only die once, but you live every day. So, stop making that sad face. You look like you're at a funeral."

"I was practicing for my upcoming role. You can hardly complain about that, now can you?" As he spoke, Thomas placed his hand on his father's shoulder.

Across the room, the waitress couldn't help but wonder about the customer who was comforting an empty chair.

9

In Carmel, a small town a little over a hundred miles south of San Francisco, crowds often gather on the beach at dusk to watch the sun slip into the ocean. But in San Francisco, dawn is the real showstopper. In the early morning hours, the Golden Gate Bridge disappears into the fog, which envelops the bay and covers the city up to the marina. Arthur had explained all of this to Thomas.

The sun rises slowly out of its cottony veil, he had said, casting a honey-colored hue on the Pacific beaches. Then, after it passes over the Castro neighborhood, the fog evaporates once more, as quickly as a receding tide.

Arthur had told Thomas that if he woke up early enough, he should go up Twin Peaks to enjoy the breathtaking view. He even had offered to lend Thomas his car. When he woke up at first light, Thomas decided to take this advice.

He left through the back door, where he caught the smell of freshly tilled soil wafting from the yard. The Saab was parked in an alley that ran along the side of the Victorian home. Thomas took Arthur's keys out of his pocket.

His father was sitting in the back seat. Raymond explained that he'd always wanted to have a chauffeur. "I couldn't have afforded it with my salary," he said. "So, it's particularly gratifying now to be driven around by my son."

"As far as I'm concerned, you can sit on the hood. I don't mind."

"Be careful when you downshift. The transmission on this car is tricky."

"Since when are you a car expert?" Thomas asked, amused.

"I had a Saab just like this one before you were born, can you believe it? I drove your mother all the way to Tuscany in it! She was a beauty, olive green—the car, not your mother, of course. Jeanne hated the color, but she liked how comfortable the seats were."

"If you hadn't met Camille, do you think you and Mom would have stayed in love?"

"If we'd been capable of loving each other for that long, I don't think Camille would have come into my life. I'll admit, I did like to flirt a little. But who could blame me for that? I wasn't a womanizer, though. I had too much respect for women to do that."

"You said things soured between you and Mom after I was born. Am I the reason you ended up getting divorced?"

"*We* were the reason. Over time, people start to take everything for granted, including their spouses. When I was your age, I promised I would never be like the men who forget the passion of a relationship's beginning, that one that dominates the first months or even years. But your mother and I did forget. We slowly grew apart, without realizing that the distance between us was growing. The affection we had for each other disappeared, and the tender, little daily gestures—which are much more important than any of us are willing to admit—vanished with it. Sometimes, I would watch as you kissed your mother good night and think, How could an adult ever love another person that much? What happened between us wasn't your fault at all. And, though it might surprise you to hear it, you proved me wrong. The love we have for our children has no bounds—it's proof that people can love unconditionally. You helped me understand that. If it weren't for you, I probably wouldn't have any hope of a second chance. Which brings us back to Camille," Raymond concluded as he slipped into the front seat. "Say, is there a problem with the car?"

"No, the engine's purring like a kitten. Why?"

"No reason. I was just wondering why we're going so slow."

Thomas shot his father a dirty look.

"Eyes on the road, please. At the speed we're going, who knows what could happen."

"So, what happened when you and Mom went to Italy?"

"Don't think about your mother now. We need to focus on the task at hand. First, we'll case the joint during the funeral. We'll take a few pictures while no one is looking. We'll need a disposable camera. Come to think of it, maybe not—the lab that develops them could connect the dots when they hear the story on the news. Unless you pay cash. Don't forget to stop by an ATM. After you take the photos, we'll draw up a detailed map that includes all possible points of entry: doors, windows, ceiling lights, and ventilation shafts. Then, later that night, we'll break in. Easy peasy."

"Easy peasy, huh?"

"More or less."

"Who do you think you are? A thief like Arsène Lupin?"

"What's wrong with Lupin? He was a gentleman, and always impeccably dressed."

"Look, they don't sell disposable cameras anymore. And we're *not* going to break in. Let me remind you that the 'us' you're referring to is actually just me. I'll go 'case' the place, as you put it, and then simply figure out the best way to go back after the funeral to get some time alone with both urns, to mix your ashes together."

"That's another way to do it," Raymond admitted. "Less exciting, but . . ."

"More practical. I think 'practical' is the word you're looking for."

"But what about scattering them?"

"Look, the terms of our absurd agreement were quite clear: I'm to mix you two together and give the whole thing a good shake. That's it."

Raymond was quiet for a moment.

"And what if her husband decides to keep us? On his nightstand, for example. Surely you can see how awkward that would be?"

"Do you know a lot of men who sleep with their dead wives on their nightstand?"

"No. But don't forget, he was an engineer."

"So?"

"Who knows how a person like that thinks! He takes things very seriously. He put over five thousand miles between Camille and me to keep us apart. If that's not over-the-top behavior, I don't know what is!"

"Stealing an urn full of still-warm ashes is one example that comes to mind."

"Thomas, don't forget you still owe me some respect. I am your father, after all."

"It's funny, you always used to say that to me when you were wrong."

"Well, then I can't have said it very often!"

When they reached the top of the hill, Thomas left the car on the road next to the park and walked the few steps to the viewpoint. A thick fog floated over the ocean like a shroud. Like a white desert drifting through the air.

"I have to admit, a man could dream of having a view like that." Raymond sighed. "But I get it if you'd rather leave me in some brass pot."

Thomas rested his gaze on a flower bed of red and white tulips planted in perfect rows. The work of a meticulous gardener. Nature was cooperative in this place. There wasn't even a single weed to throw off the symmetry.

"What we did in the plane—that is, what you helped me to do—was incredible," he said.

"Really?"

"Going onstage gives me an incredible rush; I feel a fire in my belly. But that feeling's nothing compared with what I felt the moment that man regained consciousness."

"It's funny you say that. Most of my colleagues visited their patients after they'd been taken back to their rooms. But I always preferred to see them right when they woke up from the anesthesia. I liked watching them come out of it. Whatever their age, whenever my patients opened their eyes or mumbled something as they regained consciousness, I felt like I was witnessing a birth. That moment of awakening was magical. Still, don't underestimate what you accomplish when you play. I was there at your concert, and I saw the audience light up. Their eyes were full of wonder. *Believe you me*, as your good old Albert would say."

"His name's Marcel. Tell me, why did that man pass out on the plane?"

"He must have overheard your conversation with your seatmate. No doubt it sapped him of his will to live."

"Could you be serious every once in a while?"

"How strange: When I was alive, you were always telling me to lighten up. That man was diabetic. You saved his life by giving him that injection. Whatever else happens, this trip will have resulted in some good."

"That's true." Thomas sighed. "You win, I'll scatter your ashes."

"*Our* ashes, to be clear," his father specified. "Don't forget to shave before going to the funeral home, okay? I'd like you to look your best for Camille."

"Why? Will she be able to see me?" Thomas asked worriedly.

"I don't think so. It's just the principle of the thing. Honestly, you don't see much of anything at first . . . I'd better stop there. I'll get in trouble if I say any more."

When he got back to the small Green Street apartment, Thomas did as he had been told. He took a shower, shaved, and put on a pair of jeans and a polo shirt. He was just contemplating where to get breakfast when his dad interrupted.

"I hope you aren't planning to go to the funeral home dressed like that. Change into your gray suit, please."

Thomas rifled through his bag, but it wasn't there. "I forgot it at home," he said. "I brought two button-down shirts and a pair of khakis, plus what I have on. Since I wasn't traveling for a concert for once, I just threw in the bare minimum."

"You don't have a tie?"

"No tie, no jacket. Except for the suede jacket I had on the plane."

"A suede jacket? We're not going to an air show, for heaven's sake! We'll have to buy you something decent to wear, right away. And please don't try to tell me that those things you have on your feet are supposed to pass as dress shoes."

"Do you honestly believe I can afford to buy new clothes every time I travel to a new city?"

"A dark-colored suit and a pair of loafers, there's no other way. And a tie! You'll inherit money when your mother dies," Raymond replied furiously.

"Charming. I'm sure Mom would be delighted to hear you hurrying along her death so her son can dress nicely for his father's mistress's funeral."

"Don't exaggerate. Anyway, what's the point of a credit limit if you don't use it?"

"I do use it. I'm at my limit."

"Don't they pay pianists these days?"

"They do, but not well."

Raymond slumped onto the couch. "No one attends a funeral in jeans and sneakers," he complained. "What were you thinking when you were packing?"

"I had a few teeny, tiny things on my mind. Like how I was going to get through airport security with my dad's remains, why his ghost had suddenly appeared, and how I felt about the fact that he was in love with a woman I never even knew existed. Not to mention the question of why I had agreed to steal her ashes, and—very fleetingly—what might happen if I got caught. Oh, and I almost forgot, there was also my concert in Warsaw on Saturday night. You're right, I can't believe I was so distracted I forgot to pack my best clothes."

"This sarcastic streak of yours is new," Raymond muttered. "You weren't always like that."

"You're right, this is the new me. So, what's it going to be? Am I going to break into that funeral home dressed in jeans or not at all?"

"We could just steal a suit."

"Excuse me?"

"You heard me right. While you're trying it on, I'll create a diversion, and you can run out of the store."

"Better yet, why don't we steal the hearse? It'd be easier, and it would take care of both our problems at once."

"Fantastic idea!" his father exclaimed. "All you'd have to do then is drive straight to the ocean."

"That was a joke, Dad."

"You're right; it would be too risky. Plus, her idiot husband will probably be in it, and we can't just throw him out the door while we're driving. Though I'll admit, the idea does have a certain appeal."

They heard the Triumph's wheels screech to a halt outside the house.

"Stay here," Thomas ordered. "I have a slightly less crazy idea than the ones we've been discussing. I can't promise anything, but I'll do my best."

He walked out the garage door to meet Lauren, who was just coming home from the hospital.

"Hard shift?" he asked.

"A little," she replied. "Someone got a concussion at three o'clock in the morning. People drive like maniacs, and then, when things go wrong, it's my job to fix them."

"I see," Thomas said with a glance at her car's faintly smoking tires.

It was obvious that Lauren wanted to go inside, see her husband, and enjoy a little well-deserved rest, but Thomas didn't budge from the doorway.

"Is there a problem?" she asked worriedly.

"This request will seem a little strange, but is there any chance you could rent me a suit?"

She looked at him in surprise.

"I know, it's ridiculous. I forgot mine in Paris, and what I'm wearing isn't really suitable for a funeral," he explained, gesturing toward his jeans. "I would go buy one, but my budget's pretty tight at the moment."

"I see," Lauren said. "I could ask Arthur to let you borrow one—no need to pay. You're about the same size. He has several he never wears. Come with me."

Lauren led the way to a room in which Arthur sat working at his architect's desk. He stood up to welcome his wife and then noticed Thomas standing behind her.

Thomas smiled awkwardly as Lauren rifled through the room's closet on the hunt for a suit.

"I prefer the blue one, but black seems best given the circumstances," she said as she handed it over. "Do you need anything else?"

"A tie?" Thomas ventured, lowering his eyes to the floor in embarrassment.

Arthur watched the whole thing in amusement.

"What size shoe do you wear?" he asked Thomas as Lauren walked out of the room. "I can lend you some loafers, too, if you need them."

"Size twelve, thank you. My father hates sneakers."

"Is your father in town?"

"No, sorry, force of habit. My father's been dead for a long time."

Arthur walked to the door of the room and passed Lauren on her way back in, a tie in hand.

"I'm going to get a pair of shoes," he said with a chuckle.

He returned a moment later and passed the shoes to Thomas, who thanked him and gave him back his keys.

"Was the view as beautiful as I said?"

"Even more so."

Thomas thanked them again profusely and backed out of the room, still ducking his head.

"He's certainly unique," Lauren said when he was gone.

"Seems like a nice guy," Arthur added. "You're right, though. There is something strange about him."

"You mean, like the fact that he took an eleven-hour flight to go to a funeral and forgot a suit?"

"Is he alone in the apartment?"

"He was when he got here. Why?"

"I heard him talking a few times."

"He must have been talking to himself. I do it all the time in the ER. I've been known to yell at packages of gauze that won't open. I even shout at uncooperative gurneys."

"Yes, but you're a little nuts. Not everyone is crazy in your special way, you know." Arthur kissed his wife. "It was just a feeling I got."

"What kind of feeling?"

"As if there was some sort of aura around him."

Lauren turned and headed toward their bedroom but then stopped halfway.

"What do you mean by 'some sort of aura'?"

"I don't really know how to describe it. Why are you looking at me like that?"

"No reason," Lauren said.

And then she walked out and shut the door behind her.

"Crisis averted," Raymond said with a genuine sigh of relief.

"I'll put on the suit, and then we can head to the funeral home. What's the address?" asked Thomas.

"I don't know exactly," Raymond replied. "But I know I can guide you there."

"How?"

"Just a gut feeling," he answered nonchalantly.

Raymond categorically refused to say any more after that. He said that he was afraid he'd be called back to the afterlife for sharing information the living weren't supposed to have. He promised to offer Thomas more details as they got closer to their destination.

"You chewed me out for forgetting a tie in Paris, but you don't even know where the funeral is taking place!" Thomas grumbled.

"The place is green." Raymond lifted his head calmly.

"Why are you sniffing the air?"

"I'm trying to concentrate. You're distracting me."

"Green," Thomas repeated. "Any other clues, Lassie?"

"That's enough of that! It's very green, and ostentatious. It doesn't surprise me that her husband chose a place like that."

"A place like what, may I ask? That is, if I'm not distracting you."

"I can see marble, gilt moldings, a large cupola, and lots of people. It looks like some kind of fancy mausoleum."

"So a cemetery, then?"

"No, this place is something different. I can't describe it. I've never seen anything like it."

Thomas took out his smartphone, did a quick search, and turned the screen around to face his father.

"Something like this?" he asked, pointing to the San Francisco Columbarium.

"Yes, exactly that! I found it!" Raymond exclaimed.

"*You* found it?"

"I'm telling you, Thomas, it isn't normal to be so sensitive at your age."

"One Loraine Court, that's the address. Please, don't thank me."

"My eternal thanks. Happy?"

Thomas scrolled through the photos to make sure it was the right place. The Columbarium stood in the middle of a lush park surrounded by a number of grand buildings. The most impressive of them looked a bit like the Jefferson Memorial.

"This place is huge! How am I going to find Camille in the middle of all those people?" Raymond asked.

"What people?"

"It's very strange. I can see it's not a cemetery, but there's definitely a crowd."

Thomas swiped his finger across the screen, then stopped on a picture of the Columbarium that left him dumbfounded. Various wings extended from the central dome area, all of them filled with rooms that had tiny glass cabinets covering the walls. Each compartment contained one or more urns, as well as knickknacks, pictures, and other personal effects. Each one told the story of a life.

"There actually are a lot of people in your Columbarium," Thomas confirmed. He showed the photo to his father.

"This is so stupid. I'll never find her in there," Raymond said.

"Don't be such a pessimist. I know what to do."

"What?" his father asked worriedly.

"We'll just look her up on the Dignity Memorial website. It'll tell us which building the funeral will be in. What was her last name?"

"Brrrttlll," mumbled Raymond.

"What was that?"

"Brrrttlll," he repeated.

"That's not a name."

"Bartel! It's her husband's name. Did you get it this time?"

"I'm telling you, Dad, it's not normal to be so jealous at your age."

Thomas went to the bedroom and put on the suit and tie. He then came out to show his father.

"Much better," Raymond said approvingly. "But there's still one problem. I haven't seen any subway stations around here. No bus stops, either. And the taxi that brought us here already cost you a fortune. Do you think it would be too much to ask them to borrow their car again? And go brush your hair."

"I've abused their hospitality enough already," Thomas said as he stepped into the bathroom. "I'll get an Uber."

"A what?"

"A chauffeur," Thomas replied while fixing his hair in front of the mirror.

"And all this time, you've been telling me you were broke," Raymond muttered.

The car sped down Scott Street. Ten minutes later, they arrived at the funeral home gates.

A huge mausoleum built of white stone, with exquisite stained-glass windows and a copper dome, rose up from the center of a majestic park with freshly cut grass, groves of trees and shrubbery, and brightly colored flower beds. Long, equally majestic buildings stood on either side.

"Camille would have hated this place," Raymond protested as they stepped through the gates.

"I think it's beautiful," Thomas told him.

"All this spectacle. It's nothing like her. Her husband must have chosen this place to impress other people, as usual. When the four of us used to have dinner together, he was always bragging, even though he wasn't even a millionaire at the time. His favorite topic of discussion was himself, and he could go on and on for days. He never asked anyone any questions, and he hadn't the slightest interest in others."

"He must have had a few good qualities, though. After all, Camille married him."

"A youthful mistake. Maybe you've heard of such a thing?"

"Actually, I'm pretty sure I'm committing one right now."

One look at his father's gloomy expression told Thomas that this was not the time for humor.

Raymond walked toward the Columbarium, and Thomas joined him. At the door, Thomas stopped to let his father in first, but Raymond didn't move.

"Go ahead, go in," he said. "I'll wait here."

Thomas entered the mausoleum. The combination of silence and light created an unusual atmosphere: serene, surprisingly joyous, and a little strange. The light that streamed in through the stained-glass windows created a mosaic on the floor. Six rows of varnished wooden chairs sat under the cupola, across from a modern marble altar. The rounded walls of the rotunda featured glass cabinets full of urns. Eight porticos led from the edges of the round room to more alcoves containing additional urns. Above the entrances were inscribed the names of Greek and Roman gods of the winds: Solanus, Eurus, Auster, Notus, Zephyrus, Olympus, Arktos, and Aquilo.

"Are you here to put in the lights?" said a voice behind Thomas. "The disco ball has to be installed in the center of the dome. It's really important to my father."

He turned around and saw a young woman about his age wearing black jeans, a fitted white blouse, and a cream-colored bolero jacket that added a touch of elegance to her delicate appearance.

"No, I'm not the lighting person," he replied in hesitant English.

"Sound?"

"No."

She looked at him curiously. Thomas felt an impulse to explain that he'd come to check the place out.

"Are you French?" she asked in perfect French.

"I'd have a hard time convincing you otherwise. Your French is incredible," Thomas replied.

"My parents are French . . . Well, my mother *was* French, I should say. I grew up in San Francisco, though. That's why I still have a slight accent when I speak French."

"I didn't notice one at all, and I'm a musician."

"Have you lost someone too?"

"My father."

"Which service are you doing? Dignity Memorial has so many options, it's hard to choose."

"What kind of service are you talking about?" asked Thomas, confused.

"For your father's funeral."

"Oh, his happened a long time ago," he replied, unable to lie. "It's a long story. What about you, when's your mother's funeral?"

"Tomorrow, late morning. I'm really dreading it, to be honest."

"I won't keep you, then. I'm sure you have a lot to do. It was great to meet you . . . Sorry, that didn't come out right, given the circumstances. I apologize."

"Don't worry about it. You're the first person since Mom's death who hasn't smothered me in their grief. I've just lost my mother, and all that her friends can talk about is how sad *they* are."

"I remember that," Thomas replied with a smile. "I remember consoling my father's secretary for hours while she cried on my shoulder."

"I do have to go," the young woman said, her tone apologetic. "But it was good to meet you too. It's funny, but something about your face seems familiar," she added as she held out her hand.

Thomas shook it. Before leaving, he turned back one last time. "Don't worry about tomorrow. You won't fully realize what's happening yet. That part comes later, after the phone stops ringing. That's when their absence really takes up space."

"That's comforting. Thanks for your honesty."

Thomas walked back across the park. His father was waiting for him at the gates.

"Did you get a good look around?"

"I can't do this," Thomas blurted out.

"What can't you do?"

"I agreed simply to make you happy, without thinking about the consequences—other than what would happen if I got caught. I never thought about her family. That is, I thought about her husband because I wanted to hate him as much as you do. But her daughter . . . I can't steal her mother's remains."

Raymond clasped his hands behind his back and walked down the street toward the bay. Thomas ran after him.

"Are you listening to me?"

"It's not like we're stealing a body. It's only ashes, which will get scattered anyway."

"Not if her daughter wants to keep them here, where family and friends can come pay their respects."

"You can't give up on us, Thomas. Not here, not now. Camille and I have waited so long to be together! Manon has her whole life ahead of her; our lives are behind us."

"'Manon'? You know her name?"

"Wait. I have the solution."

"I can tell I'm going to love this."

"You can just pour Camille's ashes into my urn and fill hers with sand or the dust from the apartment you're renting. A quick spin with the vacuum cleaner should give you enough to fill it up. Her daughter will be none the wiser, and she can pay her respects anytime she likes here in this tomb straight out of *The Arabian Nights*."

"Pay her respects to the contents of a vacuum cleaner bag? That's your grand idea?"

"Dust to dust. The Bible's words, not mine!"

"You'll stop at nothing, will you?"

"May I remind you that my stubbornness saved a lot of lives? Anyway, do you think parents deserve a fate like this? Did we really spend our lives raising our children only for them to put us in a tiny cabinet behind a glass door in the end? Talk about ungrateful," Raymond cried. "First the nursing home and then the urn!"

10

Thomas was sitting on the terrace of a French bakery on Arguello Boulevard. He had ordered coffee and an almond croissant, which he was now devouring.

"'Columbarium,' what a grotesque word," Raymond muttered. "'Columba' is the Latin word for 'pigeon,' did you know that? Do I look like a pigeon to you?"

"Never mind that. We need a new plan."

"It's your lucky day, then, because I have two to suggest," Raymond said. "I've been thinking about nothing else, though I have to say, it's not easy to concentrate with you wolfing down your croissant like that. I'll start with Plan B."

"Why not start with Plan A?"

"Because I know you. You'll reject the first suggestion on principle. So, here it is: You slip in and mingle discreetly with the guests. Then, when the ceremony is over, you find a way to hang back. There has to be a good hiding place or two in a building that big. When the sun goes down, you just come out of hiding, take the urn, and walk out. Simple, right?"

"What's the other plan?"

"See! What did I tell you? Plan A begins the same way. I'm sure there will be a lot of guests. Camille was a very likable person. Given her husband's vanity, he'll want to impress them all with a big reception. When people make their way to the buffet, you stay behind and transfer the ashes into my urn, leaving Camille's urn where you found it and the other people none the wiser."

"I'm getting tired of you saying 'none the wiser,'" Thomas said. "And I see you really took my moral concerns to heart."

"I thought we'd settled all that," Raymond replied in an innocent tone. "But since I apparently am wrong, how about a compromise? You can leave some of Camille's ashes in her urn. I don't think that will change anything about our fate, and that way her daughter won't be paying her respects to an empty vessel. But be careful, only leave a little bit!"

This suggestion didn't fully satisfy Thomas, but he just wanted the whole thing to be over. He swallowed his last bite of croissant, licked his fingers, and accepted with a nod.

"You're going to stain that suit if you continue on like that," his father grumbled. "Did you bring a change of clothes? Let's be tourists for a while."

The cable car made its way down California Street, the clicking sound of its rack and pinion setting a tempo. Thomas drummed his fingers in time on the wooden bench. His father stood on the step with a cheerful expression on his face, his head uncovered against the breeze—although, strangely enough, his hair didn't actually move in the wind. As Thomas studied his father, he felt certain he looked even younger than before.

The car slowed as it approached the end of the line. Raymond jumped off and began to walk quickly, gesturing for his son to follow.

"Does time run backward in your world, like a watch whose hands turn counterclockwise?" Thomas asked.

"If you're hoping to get something out of me by catching me off guard, don't waste your time. I'm not going to risk ruining everything when I'm so close to my goal. And by the way, why do you have so many questions about what's happened since I died, instead of asking about what I did with my life when I was still alive? If you want to make up for lost time and for all we left unsaid, now's the time to do it. Feel free to jump in anywhere. What would you like to know about your father?"

The question plunged Thomas into a pensive silence.

Mr. Bartel was checking the chairs to make sure they were properly aligned under the dome in the Columbarium. He pushed one an inch forward to make a perfect row.

"I don't think the people who come to Mom's funeral will notice that level of detail, Dad. It's a waste of time. And anyway, you know she always liked a little disorder."

"We complemented each other perfectly in that way," Mr. Bartel said. "I can't stand a mess."

"At least now you won't have to clean up after her anymore," Manon said.

Mr. Bartel came over and took her hand.

"Everyone grieves in their own way. You've lost your mom; I've lost my wife. I just need you to make sure everything is perfect for tomorrow. Have you met with the organ player?"

"He isn't here yet. But the equipment has been delivered. I had them set up the keyboard far enough from the altar so that people won't really see it."

"Will they still hear the music?" Mr. Bartel sounded worried.

"It's an electric organ. We can always turn up the volume."

"You didn't forget the list of the pieces we selected, did you?"

"I have the lyrics, the scores, and the order you wrote up. If it'll make you feel better, I can get a stopwatch too."

"No need. Since everything's all set, I'm going in to the office. I'm just spinning in circles here."

"The room lends itself to that, doesn't it?" Manon joked, looking up at the dome overhead.

Once her father had left, she adjusted a few chairs so they were back where they had been, re-creating the slight disorder that her mother would have wanted.

A Columbarium employee came over and introduced the organist. The man, in his sixties, was dressed in a ruffled shirt and bell bottoms that contrasted with the severe expression he apparently thought would convey his condolences. Manon gave him the list of songs and the outline of the ceremony, then stood with her back against one of the columns and settled in to listen to the rehearsal.

But as soon as he began to play, Manon felt tears welling in her eyes. She fled the mausoleum for some fresh air in the park, where the smell of newly mowed grass revived her.

She was dreading the evening ahead of her almost as much as she was the next day's funeral. If she had dinner with her father, the silence would push her right over the edge. She'd have to swallow her pride and call a friend to rescue her. A girls' night with a little alcohol—make that a lot of alcohol—would do her good. Her mother would definitely have wanted Manon to have fun, rather than mope around.

"Do you remember things better, now that you're up there?" she whispered, her face directed toward the sky. "I really hope death has fixed your memory. After you're in your final resting place here, I'll come sit with you and tell you about all the times we spent together, just like I've done the past few years. I know you're still here in a way. I feel your presence. I'll tell you about my childhood, the feeling of your hands stroking my face, of your kisses showering me with love, of your reassuring words. Your joy and spontaneity that brightened my life. I'll tell you about our alfresco lunches, about how we shared all our secrets, the times we burst out laughing, the times we disagreed. I'll have to live without you for so long, Mom. I'm not going to speak at the service tomorrow. Please don't be angry with me. I just can't do it. It's too painful, and the words I have to say are only for you, anyway. For the two of us. See you tomorrow, Mom."

Manon walked back toward the Columbarium with a heavy heart. She stepped into the mausoleum to find the organist sorting his music. She nodded her goodbye as he left, then arranged a bouquet on the altar and sat down in the last row to admire it all.

As Thomas strolled down Market Street, he stopped in front of an optician's window to admire a pair of sunglasses. He jumped when he saw his father reflected in the glass wearing a pair of 1940s vintage-style Ray-Bans.

"What do you think? It's for tomorrow."

"How did you do that?" asked Thomas, staring at the glasses.

"I don't know. I discover a new ability with each passing minute. It's pretty fun. I have to be careful, though. When we walked past that costume shop earlier, I was reminded of a costume party your mother and I had gone to. We had a great time. But I almost ended up with a wig back there. You would have given me one of your scolding looks. Anyway, should I keep the glasses or not?"

"It seems a little late to be wondering that."

"I'm asking you if they look good on me."

"It's the perfect look for an air show. I can even lend you my suede jacket."

Raymond pushed the glasses down his nose and shot his son a dirty look over the lenses.

"You look very handsome," Thomas said, more charitably this time.

"I owned the same ones when I met your mother. Would you like to hear how we met?"

"I've heard the story a hundred times, but I'm happy to hear it again."

"You don't know the real story," Raymond replied before launching into the tale of how he won Jeanne's heart. "I was a resident at Boucicaut Hospital. One night, when I was working in the emergency room, they brought in a young man who was in terrible shape. He'd had a motorcycle accident. It was summer, and a lot of the doctors were on vacation, so I had to operate solo for the first time. I did my best, but it wasn't enough; he died on the table. That first patient I lost had an impact on the rest of my life—it's almost ironic, when you think about it. It fell to me to tell his family. I took off my gloves, my surgical cap and gown, and I made my way to the waiting room. But there wasn't any family there to speak to, just a young woman alone on a bench. I noticed her right away because she was strikingly beautiful. When she looked up, I realized she was there for my patient. When I shared the news, she took it with remarkable dignity, not showing any outward signs of emotion. She thanked me and left. But at the end of my shift, I found her outside, curled up against a wall and crying every single tear from her body. She'd spent the whole night out there. I have no idea why, but I walked over and asked her to follow me in an authoritative tone. She got in my car—a Simca eleven hundred I should never have given up—and we drove all the way to Trouville without exchanging a single word. I parked in front of Les Vapeurs restaurant, and we ordered two crepes, which we ate while gazing into each other's eyes, still without breaking the silence. We didn't say a word throughout the entire meal, or during the two-hour drive home, either. When I dropped her off in front of her building, she simply thanked me again. Funny story, huh?"

"Your definition of the word 'funny' doesn't always line up with mine, but I will admit it's an interesting way for two people to meet. What happened next?"

"Ah, I'm delighted to see you're finally interested in your old dad's life."

"It was Mom's life, too, right?"

"Yes, of course. Anyway, three years went by. It was March twenty-first—I remember because it was the first day of spring. I was supposed to attend a charity cocktail party; I had promised weeks before that I would go. But when the time came, I had no desire to keep my word. Fortunately, a pang of last-minute regret got me there. The event was taking place on the top floor of the Théâtre des Champs-Élysées. I was standing there, admiring the view, when your mother appeared in a red dress that fell just above her knees. She was breathtakingly beautiful, and I couldn't help but stare. She smiled, then disappeared into the crowd. Your mother knew immediately that I hadn't recognized her; don't ask me how—a woman's instinct is more of a mystery than creation itself. In my defense, she looked nothing like the tearful young woman I had driven to Normandy. Much time had passed. For over an hour, we played a game of cat and mouse. I would walk toward a table where she was chatting with friends, and just before I got there, she would get up and move to another. Whenever I neared the bar, where she was waiting for a drink, she would go back to her seat. Then finally, suddenly, I heard a voice behind me say, 'You have no idea who I am, do you?' You should know that your becoming a pianist didn't come out of nowhere. You got your musical ear from me. Though my memory for faces is atrociously bad, I have never, ever forgotten a voice. And I especially did not forget the voice of the woman who had thanked me twice in that grave and melodious tone. Without turning around, I answered, 'Maybe a chocolate crepe and a seaside view would jog my memory.' It's a real blow to my ego to admit this, but I actually won your mother's heart with that idiotic line."

"Now, *that* I would call funny," Thomas said. "Go on."

"We exchanged numbers—landlines, because mobile phones only existed in the cars of government officials back then. I called her two days later only to learn she was heading out the door to go to Biarritz for a story. At the time, your mother worked for *Paris Match.* She promised to call when she got back, but she called from her hotel instead. It was a Friday. She'd been writing her article in a beachside bar and would be coming home Sunday. She suggested we have dinner together then. Since the only restaurants open on Sunday were terribly depressing places in train stations or tourist traps, I invited her to my small apartment on Rue de Bretagne. I went to the market in the morning and spent the whole afternoon cooking. Around five o'clock, the phone rang again. Your mother said she was afraid the traffic around Orly Airport would be terrible on a Sunday night, and she'd decided to come back the next day instead."

"What did you do?" Thomas asked.

"I had dinner for one and remained as calm and composed as she'd been the first two times we met. I was sure that was the end of it."

"But it wasn't . . ."

"Brilliant observation, son. You wouldn't be here if it had been. The next day, as I was leaving for work, I found a small package on my welcome mat. It was a Basque cake wrapped in parchment paper, upon which your mother had written that she hoped I'd have a good day."

"So, she came home on Sunday night after all?"

"Obviously."

"I don't understand."

"Which only proves that you have a lot to learn about women. She didn't want our first date to take place with just the two of us in my apartment."

"So, what did you do after you found the cake?"

"I ate it during my shift."

"I mean, what did you do about Mom! Did you call her?"

"Better. I sent her flowers at work."

"Not bad. Romantic, even."

"No, not romantic. Vengeful and calculating. Sending them to her office was a refined way of getting her back. Can you imagine what her colleagues must have said when the bouquet showed up?"

"Why calculating?"

"Because I knew those same colleagues would try all week to get information out of her about the man who had sent the flowers. There was no way she could forget me, even if she wanted to! My ploy worked. We saw each other again soon, and after that first date, we were inseparable."

"Up until the summer you met Camille, you mean," Thomas corrected him.

"Fifteen years later. And I don't regret a single day I spent with your mother."

Thomas turned toward his father and noticed he was staring strangely at him.

"What is it?" he asked.

"Look behind me," said Raymond.

When Thomas did, he noticed the facade of San Francisco's Davies Symphony Hall, one of the most beautiful concert halls in the world.

"Why do you think I've dragged myself all over the city telling you my life story? If I'd told you where I was taking you, you would have said no. Come on, let's go in."

"It's a lovely gesture, but a person can't just walk into a place like that."

"How do you know? Whenever I traveled, I loved visiting hospitals and seeing where my colleagues worked. Your lack of curiosity worries me, son."

Thomas walked over to read the poster hanging on one of the columns: "Daniel Harding, Mikhail Pletnev conducting the Russian National Orchestra, Anne-Sophie Mutter, Jean-Yves Thibaudet . . ." The list of concerts scheduled for the next several weeks made him imagine himself performing there one day.

He pushed through the door.

The lobby was empty, except for a single employee at the ticket counter.

"I really must teach you to be stealthier," his father said under his breath. "Ask him if you can visit the auditorium. Introduce yourself. A renowned French musician visiting San Francisco. I'm sure he'll let you go in."

"I'm just a pianist, and hardly a renowned one," Thomas protested.

"Not yet you aren't. Now, come on. Make your old man proud."

The employee asked Thomas to wait a moment and then picked up the phone. Within minutes, the public relations manager came down. Just as Raymond had predicted, he was delighted to give Thomas a tour.

As they walked, the man asked Thomas about his career—an elegant way to make sure he wasn't a fake. Thomas spoke about his most recent concerts, and to his great surprise, the PR manager told him he'd heard great things about Thomas's interpretation of Mozart's Piano Concerto No. 23 at the performance he'd given in Stockholm in December, which the queen had attended.

"I can't tell you how nervous I was when I learned that Queen Silvia would be there," Thomas told him humbly.

The man took him through the backstage area to the main stage, which looked out over twenty-seven hundred seats. He proudly explained that the concave panels hanging from the ceiling were modular sound reflectors that could change the acoustics of the auditorium to suit the composition, the orchestra, and even the audience. Thomas couldn't help but think that Marcel would find it all extraordinary.

"The wall hangings on either side can also be removed," the PR manager added. "We can even modify the reverb. I would have loved to let you try out all these marvels of modern technology, but the engineers are already hard at work on tonight's concert. Now come with me. I have one last thing to show you."

Thomas followed the man, and his father trailed behind him with an admiring look on his face. They left the stage via a door on the opposite side and headed down a hallway to an adjacent building.

"We have two auditoriums for rehearsals, which are also worth seeing," the PR manager explained as he stopped in front of a light oak door.

Inside, Thomas was surprised yet again. The rehearsal room was big enough for a full philharmonic orchestra.

"Impressive, right? It was designed to allow ballet companies to rehearse under performance conditions."

The auditorium wasn't just big—it was huge. A Bösendorfer sat resplendent in the middle of the stage. Thomas preferred Bösendorfers to Steinways because of the matchless depth of their lower octaves.

"Try it out," the man offered.

Thomas didn't need to be told twice. It had been three days since he'd touched a keyboard. He sat down on the bench and warmed up with Ravel's "Jeux d'eau" before moving on to a couple of Chopin's études—the first, in C major, followed by the twelfth, in C minor. The PR manager was clearly enjoying his personal concert.

When he was done, Thomas reluctantly stood up and thanked his guide for allowing him to play.

"Come see us again sometime. We host musicians from all over the world. Our audiences enjoy seeing new faces. We've even had several French artists, including Ms. Hélène Grimaud, who will be playing here at the end of the month." Thomas's eyes widened upon hearing the name of the esteemed pianist.

"Are you serious?" he said to the man. Though his father's arm passed through Thomas's as he elbowed him, Thomas could still feel it.

"If you're interested, I'll give you my contact information." The PR manager held out his business card. Then he accompanied Thomas to the stage door and shook his hand.

"So?" Raymond asked. "Who was right this time? You see, I can help you out too. If that offer pans out, we'll be even!"

On the way back to the house on Green Street, Raymond mentioned he was surprised that the "chauffeur" didn't look like the one they'd had that morning. Even stranger, the car had changed too.

As they neared St. Patrick Church, Thomas noticed a hearse parked outside. He turned abruptly toward his father. "There are some big problems with your plan."

"I don't see any. It's perfect. But if you prefer Plan B, I'm okay with that."

"A and B both start the same way. Either way, I have to blend in with the other guests."

"Unless you want to take the priest's place, I see no alternative. But I still don't see the problem."

"I can't be incognito now that I've met Manon. She'll recognize me and wonder why I decided to crash her mother's funeral."

"Why did you have to introduce yourself to her?" Raymond complained.

"Probably because you sent me in alone to check the place out, remember?"

"All right, fine. So, you ran into each other. She'll have forgotten all about you by tomorrow. Believe me, she has other things on her mind at the moment."

"Well, we also talked . . ."

"How much did you talk, exactly?" Raymond fumed, crossing his arms.

"I don't know. We had a short conversation."

"I sincerely hope you didn't flirt with Camille's daughter."

"You're hardly one to talk. And, no, it was nothing like that. She surprised me while I was in the room and wanted to know what I was doing there. What was I supposed to do, run away?"

"You can't have said anything memorable, though. It was just small talk, right? She's probably spoken to dozens of people over the past few days. Funeral home employees, florists, caterers. I'm sure you're worried over nothing. She won't remember you."

"I'm not so sure," Thomas sighed.

"What exactly did you say? Don't leave anything out, please, Thomas!"

"I told her not to be too worried about the funeral, that the real flood of grief comes later and lasts much longer."

Raymond looked thoughtfully at his son.

"Was that you speaking from personal experience, or are you just saying that now to try to make up for your giant mistake?"

Thomas just turned toward the window.

"Fine. Don't tell me. In any case, I don't know what your superego was thinking, but I'm quite sure your ego was hitting on her. And what's worse, it sounds like he did a terrible job."

The car dropped them off on Green Street, where they found the hood of the Saab wide open and Arthur studying the engine. Thomas walked over to him.

"Did it break down?"

"No, but it backfires every time I accelerate. I can't figure out why."

"I'd love to help you, but—"

"It's the fuel pump," Raymond whispered.

"Maybe the spark plugs are bad," Arthur theorized as he stood up. "I'll take it to the garage. Such bad timing. We're going out tonight, and I'd rather not use the Triumph. What were you saying?"

"Take out the fuel line, clean it by blowing through it, and put it back in," Raymond explained confidently. "Don't look at me like that, all suspicious-like. I drove a Saab nine hundred for years, though it goes without saying that mine was in better shape."

Thomas repeated what his father had suggested.

"The fuel line? Why not. Any idea where to find it?" asked Arthur.

"Here," Raymond replied as he pointed. "My God, if I could just do it myself, he'd already be on the highway."

"It's right here," Thomas explained impassively.

Arthur got his tools from his workbench, loosened the bolts, did as Raymond had advised, and put the line back in. Then he sat down behind the wheel.

"He needs to pump the gas, or it won't start," Raymond cut in again.

"Make sure you pump the gas," Thomas advised.

Arthur turned the key in the ignition, and the engine purred, then roared as he revved the engine.

"Fantastic! You just saved my whole night."

"It was no big deal," Thomas replied.

"No, really! You saved my night and my day tomorrow, too, which I would have spent going from garage to garage, getting estimates. Right now, we're going out to dinner with friends. Would you like to come along?"

Thomas hesitated. Jet lag was taking its toll, but Arthur insisted.

"Go have some fun with people your age," Raymond urged. "I'll take advantage of the quiet to think about how to fix your little blunder. But don't come home too late. We have to be ready in the morning by nine. Suit and tie, freshly shaven, hair combed!"

Thomas was itching to tell his father he wasn't ten years old anymore, but he decided to hold his tongue in front of Arthur.

Raymond turned toward the house and walked straight through the closed door.

Arthur opened the passenger door so Thomas could climb in.

"I have to pick up Lauren from the hospital, then we'll go directly to the restaurant. You'll like our friends. Paul was my business partner once upon a time, but he's a writer now. And you might know his girlfriend—the English actress Mia Barrow. Plus, they just so happened to meet in Paris. Paul lived there for several years. You'll have plenty to talk about."

Raymond watched as the Saab started down Green Street, his face pressed to the window. Once the car was out of view, he made his way back to the Columbarium.

11

The table brought together longtime friends and a new guest.

Though the Californian accent is fairly neutral, the conversations jumped around so quickly that Thomas had a hard time following all of them. He didn't mind, though; he was used to spending time with people whose languages he didn't speak. For the sake of appearances, he smiled every now and again, nodded, or opened his eyes wide with interest.

Paul kept glancing furtively at a piano that stood against one of the walls.

"Do you play?" Thomas asked.

"Yes, I started very young. I rented a piano when I was living in Paris, but I never played it. My heart wasn't in it then. I started up again when we moved back here."

"What neighborhood did you live in?" Thomas asked, making polite conversation.

"Rue de Bretagne. But I spent most of my time in Montmartre—so inspiring."

"What a small world! My dad used to live on that street. Arthur tells me you're a writer."

"Supposedly. But I haven't made any progress on my manuscript in months."

"Why not?"

"I'm madly in love with Mia, and as if that weren't bad enough, we're happy."

"I see," Thomas replied.

"My editor won't leave me alone. On a night like tonight, I should be sitting at my desk, but I always find an excuse to do something else. I'm afraid to finish it and even more afraid that people will read it. But that's enough about me. Are you traveling for work?"

"No," Thomas said hesitantly. "I'm actually here for my father."

"Who lived on Rue de Bretagne! He's in San Francisco now?"

"He's no longer with us, but he wanted his ashes scattered at Golden Gate Park."

Paul took a notebook out of his pocket and started jotting something down. "Go ahead. Tell me more," he said, chewing on the end of his pen. "You've given me an idea." Paul seemed to be waiting for Thomas to continue, his eyes focused on the paper.

"You don't want to know. That's only the tip of the iceberg. And no one would believe any of it, unless they're into ghost stories."

"Clearly, you have no idea who you're talking to. I could have gotten a doctorate in ectoplasm studies with all I know about the subject. But what's all this about ghosts? Is your father haunting you?"

"You could say that, yes."

"That's fantastic!" Paul exclaimed. "A father returned from the great beyond to work out differences with his loved ones. I'm telling you, now *that's* a story."

"If you say so. You're the writer."

Paul stared at Thomas and put away his pen. "I'm sorry, that was inappropriate of me."

"Don't worry, I'm not offended. You keep looking over at that piano. You should go play."

"Yes, why not?" Paul agreed. "Mia would love that. Should I play some jazz or something classical?"

"Classical music might spoil the atmosphere."

Paul winked knowingly at Thomas as he sat down on the piano bench. He uncovered the keys and began a ragtime number, turning toward his friends to see if they were listening.

They had in fact all gone quiet, as had several other tables, whose occupants were now focused on Paul. But not Lauren. She was looking at Thomas. "Do you play too?" she asked, leaning toward him.

"What makes you think that?"

"Your fingers have been drumming on the table ever since Paul started this little tune."

Thomas nodded.

"Will you play something for us?"

"I'd rather not," Thomas replied.

"Why? We're all friends here."

"Because this moment belongs to your friend. He's doing quite well, in fact."

"Are you really that good?"

Thomas glanced over at Mia, who was listening rapturously to Paul's song.

"Didn't she star in an English comedy? I forget what it was called, but I saw it four or five years ago, in London."

"Did you live in London then?" asked Lauren.

"No, it was just a short stay for work."

"Speaking of which, what exactly do you do?"

"How did Paul and Mia meet, anyway?"

"Do you always answer a question with another question?"

"Not always, but often."

"Why?" asked Lauren.

"Now you're doing it, I see," Thomas said. "I'm not just being nosy, I promise. Actors travel a lot; so do musicians. I was in love with a violinist at the time, but I wasn't able to maintain a long-distance relationship."

"Paul and Mia met because of that movie," Lauren said. "Don't mention it to her, though. It brings up unpleasant memories. Her on-screen partner was also her partner in real life, but his loyalty was pure fiction. You didn't hear that from me, though."

"And since I'm deaf, I suppose Lauren's secret is safe," Mia cut in, turning toward them. "I had gone to Montmartre and taken refuge in my best friend's restaurant in Paris. Paul was one of her regulars. And since we have no more secrets between us, let me give you a little friendly advice. If you're in love with a woman who travels, travel with her. That's what I do with Paul."

"Would you mind if I bowed out a bit early?" Thomas asked. "I'm exhausted and have a big day tomorrow."

He took out his wallet, but Arthur waved a hand in the air, indicating that there was no need.

Outside, the night was cool and the sky full of stars. Thomas decided to walk back to the house on Green Street. He needed some time alone to think, and the half-hour stroll would do him a lot of good.

Raymond was pacing the Columbarium, taking in every tiny detail, just as he had always done before operating.

"I don't like saying it, but I have to admit your husband knew you very well," he said. He tried unsuccessfully to inhale the scent of a bouquet of wild roses that crowned the altar. "They barely have much of a scent, anyway, so I don't mind that my sense of smell is gone," he grumbled.

He walked up the aisle and sat down in the last row, to get an idea of what Camille's guests would see the next day.

"This is a waste of time. Even if Thomas showed up last and sat way back here, Manon would eventually notice him. Think harder, old man, it's tomorrow or never."

He surveyed the room from the altar to the front door, his gaze halting on a chair reserved for Camille's husband. He glanced past the front row to the electric organ, then to the door once more, before returning to the organ.

"Not the priest's place, no. But this could do the trick," he concluded, quite pleased with himself.

He stood up and ran his hands over the creases of his pants. As he did so, it occurred to him that not even death had put a stop to his old habits.

It turned out that he hadn't wasted his evening after all. Feeling pleased, he happily walked right through the wall.

What use was there in doing things the same old way?

Raymond reappeared in Thomas's room, then sat at the foot of the bed, looking down at his son.

"Are you asleep?" he whispered. "I found a solution to our little problem. We'll need to leave a bit earlier than planned. A little before nine o'clock, at the latest. Should I wake you in the morning?"

Since he received no reply, Raymond moved closer to the pillow and whispered: "When you were little, you always pretended to be asleep when I came to tuck you in before I went to bed. You would close your eyes so tightly that I had to bite my lip to keep from laughing. I didn't want to ruin the moment, given how much effort you put into it. You would often forget to turn off your flashlight, and the light would shine through the sheets. So, I'd go back to my office to read and wait for you to finally drift off, then come back and take it from you. You know, Thomas, if I could stay longer, if I were allowed, I would make Camille wait. I missed you so much during the last years of my life. I'll miss you even more now."

Raymond kissed Thomas's forehead and placed his hands on the top edge of the sheet. Sadly, he found that he was unable to tuck his son in.

12

"Why are we leaving so early?" Thomas asked as he knotted his tie.

"Because," replied his father tersely.

"Feeling impatient?"

"I've waited more than twenty years for this. I don't think impatient is the right word."

"Nervous, then?"

"Wouldn't you be, in my place? Go ahead, laugh at my expense, but I still remember your face when that Sophie turned up in your dressing room."

"Fine, but the service doesn't start for another two hours. Waiting outside the front door isn't the best tactic if we want to be discreet."

"That's just it. I don't want you to be discreet. Instead of sneaking in, you're going to be invited."

"Just what planet do you live on? Sorry, I didn't mean it that way. But, seriously, no one invites strangers to their mother's funeral. It's not a surprise party."

"Just wait until we get there. You'll see. Trust me."

"Do I really have a choice? Besides, I like this better. This way, if your plan fails, at least I won't have to be rude."

Raymond looked at his son, a little smirk on his face.

"Rude to who?" he asked.

"To Camille's daughter, for starters."

"Manon, you mean. Did you forget her name?"

"Fine. Manon, if you prefer."

"Oh, it makes no difference to me."

"All right, well, let's go, then. There's no point in standing around and guessing what will happen."

"There's one detail we have to take care of first," Raymond said. "And it's an important one. How are you going to transport my urn? Not in a shopping bag again, I hope!"

Thomas looked around. His suitcase was too big and would attract attention. He went into the bedroom and rifled through the closets.

"I found something," he told his father as he made his way back to the living room. He was carrying a canvas bag emblazoned with the logo of a bookstore.

Raymond complained that it was too plain for the task at hand.

"It's not plain, it's discreet. Anyway, it's not like you'll be stuck in it forever," Thomas reminded him.

Raymond checked to make sure the bag was clean on the inside, then agreed, since time was ticking away.

The car dropped them off in front of the park gates. Thomas walked down the path and stopped about fifty yards from the Columbarium.

"What do we do now?" he asked.

"We go for a stroll," his father replied.

"A stroll?"

"You're a little young to be losing your hearing, aren't you? Yes, a stroll. You put one foot in front of the other. It's not that complicated."

"But where? And don't talk to me like that. Remember, I could be enjoying a quiet week at home in Paris instead of 'strolling' about, as you put it."

"Maybe. But that would be deadly boring."

"And you think this place is so full of life?"

"Don't just stand there in one place. It looks strange. Go sit on that bench and play with your phone or count sheep if you prefer. Whatever you do, just act natural. That's all I ask."

Thomas shot his father a dirty look and went to sit on a bench in the middle of the lawn, across from the mausoleum. He took out his phone and checked his messages. Serge had sent a message informing Thomas that his girlfriend had moved back in, but that they'd fought again the night before. Philippe had shared more news from the filming of his commercial. He said he wanted to show Thomas the dailies. Thomas's mother was worried because she couldn't reach him and wanted to know if he'd left on tour without stopping to say goodbye.

"They didn't give up, either." Raymond chuckled as he appeared next to his son.

"Who are you talking about?"

"The people who designed the bench you're resting your rear end on. It's an urn of sorts, if you can believe it. I bet they mixed ashes with the concrete. This poor Gerald fellow is stuck in that bench for eternity. Here, look at the plaque; I'm not making it up. Read it for yourself."

Thomas leaned over to read the inscription on the bench.

IN LOVING MEMORY OF
GERALD FILMOORE (1949–2008)
REST IN PEACE

"Maybe he spent his whole life standing up," Raymond mused.

Thomas raised his eyes to see Manon looking his way from the entrance to the mausoleum.

"I think I've been spotted," he whispered.

"About time," his father replied, sounding relieved.

"She's staring right at me," Thomas fretted.

Manon walked over and stopped in front of the bench, then asked if she could sit down. Looking overwhelmed, she twisted her hands together without saying a word. Thomas remained quiet, hesitant to speak first.

"Did you find what you were looking for?" she finally asked, breaking the silence.

"To be honest, I don't know what I'm looking for here."

He had hoped to make her smile, but he was unsuccessful.

"Is something wrong?" Thomas asked.

"I'm burying my mom. Everything's perfect."

"Was that sarcasm? Of course it was."

"As if losing her wasn't hard enough, now I have to carry out her last wishes. She put me in charge of them instead of my father! You'd think that a parent could at least try to make their child's life a little bit easier when it comes to their death."

"Amen," Thomas said.

"I'm sorry to be so direct, but I'm in a bit of a hurry. Am I right in remembering that you told me you were a musician? What instrument do you play?"

"I'm a pianist."

"You're a godsend!"

"I promise, *God* isn't the one who sent me . . ."

"I don't want you to feel like I'm taking advantage of you, but I have a huge favor to ask." Manon turned toward him. "I'll pay you, of course."

"What kind of favor?"

"The organist we hired had some sort of an attack this morning. Today of all days!"

"Now he's dead too?"

"No, not that kind of attack, more like a sudden onset of dementia. His partner said he screamed while he was in the bathroom, then ran out, shouting as if he were being chased by the devil, and then fell. His leg is broken, and he has a concussion. So, is there any chance you could fill in at the last minute? I don't understand why you're smiling."

"A broken leg, huh? I'm sorry. It's a nervous tic."

Thomas glanced at his father, who was fiddling with his cuticles and doing a poor job of hiding his satisfaction.

"No need to give me a dirty look," Manon protested. "I'm only asking because I don't have any other options. My father is going to be very upset!"

"So is mine, but that will come a little later."

"I thought he was—"

"Where is your father now?" asked Thomas.

"He's attending the cremation." Manon gestured toward the other end of the park, where the roof of an isolated building rose up from behind an evergreen hedge. "I couldn't bear it," she added quietly.

"I'll do it," Thomas said. "But I won't let you pay me. What would you like me to play?"

Manon unexpectedly rested her head on his shoulder a moment, her eyes filled with tears. Thomas didn't dare take her hand. Instead, he pulled out a pack of tissues and held them out to her.

"Here."

Manon wiped her eyes and looked closely at him for a second.

"What is it?" Thomas asked.

"A feeling of déjà vu. Come on, I'll show you where to go."

They started toward the mausoleum. Raymond followed, lighter on his feet than ever. Halfway there, Thomas doubled back to get the canvas bag he'd forgotten at the foot of the bench.

Manon had accompanied Thomas to the organ, then abruptly abandoned him. The arrival of the first guests had cut short her explanation of the funeral schedule. Luckily, the organist had left his music on the stand in the correct order, alongside a page detailing the cues for the pieces he was to play. Thomas would have liked to practice first, but a crowd was already gathering under the dome. He leaned over the keyboard and studied the various buttons used to change the sound output. Violins, trumpet, guitar, clarinet, percussion, and oboe . . . the electric organ could simulate the sounds of an entire orchestra. Thomas selected the button for grand piano and played a perfect chord.

"Not bad," he mumbled as he adjusted the volume.

His foot touched the fabric bag containing his father's urn, which he then quickly hid behind the altar before returning to his place. He continued to familiarize himself with the new instrument by gently touching the keys, as quietly as possible.

The room had filled up. The guests stood in front of their chairs, silently paying their respects. Manon was watching the door. Her light dress fluttered in the breeze. Then she turned her red eyes to Thomas and gestured that it was time to begin.

The first piece he played was Debussy's "Clair de lune," and since he'd played it so many times before, he performed from memory. His fingers moved gracefully, solemnly accompanying Camille's ashes as they were carried into the mausoleum. Mr. Bartel handed the urn to his daughter, who placed it on the altar. Then he made his way to the podium and delivered a pompous reading of Lamartine.

What good these valleys, these cottages, these palaces,
Vain objects that for me have lost their charm and grace,
These rivers, rocks, and forests, solitudes once so dear,
A single person is missing, and all becomes a barren waste!

Whether the sun's journey is beginning or ending,
I follow its course with an indifferent gaze;
In cloudy sky, or in brilliant azure, it may set or rise,
What matters the sun? I expect nothing from days.

"Dear friends, we are gathered here today to accompany my wife to her final resting place . . ."

Thomas took advantage of the speech to look for his father. Raymond was sitting in the third row, his eyes focused on the altar, visibly moved.

As Mr. Bartel's speech was drawing to a close, Thomas checked the schedule. He put away the first piece of sheet music and was surprised when he saw the second behind it.

"Huh. Vivaldi's *Gloria* on the piano?"

Remembering that his instrument was more like a synthesizer than a Steinway, he pushed the "Violins" button, curious to hear the result. He was not disappointed. The chords he played on the keyboard set an ensemble of violins playing different parts in perfect harmony. Thomas delivered a spirited rendition, perfectly mastering the piece's jolting rhythm. Right when the choir would have made its entrance, the guests stood up and started singing, "Gloria, Gloria, Gloria, Gloria in excelsis Deo," as if they'd done it a thousand times before.

Hearing them, Thomas played even more enthusiastically. He felt like he was conducting an orchestra—one of his longest-held dreams—and the result was so magnificent that, at the end of the piece, the entire audience applauded. Out of habit, he stood up from his bench and bowed respectfully, despite Mr. Bartel's angry scowl.

Next, one of Camille's oldest friends came to the front to say a few words. He spoke of her in tender, admiring, even humorous terms and said that he was convinced she was watching them from "up there."

Thomas stopped listening as he placed the third piece on his stand. He froze upon reading the first measures. He quickly made a small gesture in Manon's direction, then a series of larger gestures to get her attention.

"I think the pianist is calling you," a guest whispered loudly.

Manon waved back, then realized Thomas actually needed her. As Camille's friend continued his speech, she got up discreetly and joined Thomas.

"I think there must be a mistake for the next piece . . ."

"No, not at all. This is exactly what we planned."

Thomas looked back to the sheet music. "'Stayin' Alive'? Really?"

"Sorry, I didn't get a chance to warn you. Mom wanted her funeral to be full of joy, like she was. Like the second-line parades in New Orleans with the brass bands, where the music carries you off to another world. Or like another life, in which all your dreams come true. Mom wasn't a big fan of jazz, but she loved disco music. I know the choice is a little unorthodox. My father didn't want to do it, but I insisted, and her friends backed me up, so he gave in. Don't worry. Everything will be fine. And you're playing great—bravo. It's been perfect."

When Manon returned to her place, Thomas—who, until that point, had been focused on the music—belatedly noticed that the guests had removed their everyday coats, revealing the surprising, retro-style outfits they'd worn underneath.

A woman in the second row was wearing a 1970s jumpsuit; her neighbor was dressed in green bell-bottoms. Further down the row sat a guy in an orange shirt with a huge collar, paired with bright-blue pants and leg warmers. To the left, Thomas saw a woman in a bell-sleeve hippie dress and, behind her, a man in a silver shirt under a plaid suit jacket. A few rows back, a man wore a ruffled top with silver sequins. A pair of neon leggings jutted out into the center aisle. Scattered around the room were gold gloves, huge thick-rimmed glasses, sequined ties, bright fedoras, and shiny baseball caps. It was like Halloween.

"What were you saying earlier? Oh yes, that we weren't going to a surprise party," his father joked, sitting on the altar.

The disco ball started spinning in the center of the dome, projecting its shimmering lights on the walls and stained-glass windows. The urns in the glass cabinets sparkled as it turned.

Thomas shook his head in amazement. "When she said Dignity Memorial had a wide selection of services, she wasn't kidding," he said.

But he was there to replace the organist and play whatever songs Manon had requested, so that's exactly what he did. He was surprised one more time, however, when the guests pushed back their chairs and started dancing to "YMCA."

Mr. Bartel danced, too, and even Raymond joined the crowd, swinging his hips as his son looked on, astounded. His father winked back gleefully.

The ambiance was unbelievable. Thomas played song after song from the sheet music in front of him: "Let's All Chant," "Just an Illusion," "Hang On in There Baby," "Ring My Bell," "Don't Leave Me This Way," "Heaven Must Have Sent You," "I'm So Excited," and—the big finale—"I Will Survive."

Then, when they'd reached the end, the guests gathered before the altar, across from the urn, and applauded loudly as they all threw their hats, scarves, and caps high into the air.

13

The party was over, and the guests were leaving the mausoleum, on their way to a reception hall with a full buffet. As they exited, Thomas took his time putting the sheet music in order, eager to be alone.

Raymond was waiting outside. He'd claimed that this was so he could be a lookout, but the truth was, he was afraid his nerves would cause him to mess up their mission, and he didn't want to watch his son do the very thing that he had asked him to do.

When the last conversations had faded into the distance, Thomas walked over to the altar.

He had to be quick. Open Camille's urn, grab his father's, which he'd hidden, transfer the ashes, and walk out as discreetly as possible.

He placed his hand on the lid, wondering if he needed to lift it off or unscrew it. But a small amount of upward pressure proved to be enough to pull it free.

"What are you doing?" Manon asked.

Thomas jumped. He hadn't heard her come in. He quickly pushed the lid back into place, but he wasn't able to close it properly, so he turned around toward her, using his body to shield the urn from view.

"I was paying my respects to your mother," he said awkwardly.

"That's very kind, thank you. But I still need you."

"To play?"

"No, I don't need a pianist. I need you. I can't take being alone in the middle of all those people."

"Do you want me to take you home?"

"I'd love that, but my father would kill me if I left. Would you mind keeping me company instead? You don't even need to talk to me, just stay by my side so people will stop coming to offer their condolences. I'm at my wits' end."

"I promise to stick to you until the guests have finished all of the hors d'oeuvres. If they stay longer than that, we'll have to improvise."

"This is going to sound strange, but I really feel like I've met you before."

Thomas kept quiet.

"Okay, that was a terrible line, I admit it," Manon said.

"Don't worry about it. Come on, your father is waiting for you, and I haven't eaten all morning. Let's hit that buffet."

The guests had gathered in a large, brightly colored room. A huge portrait of Camille hung over the mantel of an artificial fireplace. She looked to be about fifty in the photograph. It was the first time that Thomas had really looked at the face of the woman his father had fallen madly in love with, the woman he had maintained a romance with, mostly through letters, for over twenty years.

Manon had just finished making a plate with an assortment of hors d'oeuvres, and she hurried over to Thomas before a pretentious-looking older lady wearing an anguished expression could get too close.

"Your mother was beautiful," he said, picking up a macaron.

"I think she was lovely—which is much better than pretty. Beauty fades, but she always kept her smile, even after the rest of her was pretty much gone. Mom left us long before she died. In her final months, she kept calling me 'miss.' She thought I was the nurse or the cleaning lady. On really bad days, she even thought I was my father's daughter by another woman. She would scream that I couldn't take her daughter's place even if she *was* ungrateful and neglectful of her mother. And then at other times, a light would come into her eyes, and I felt like she recognized me, though she didn't say so. Now I can finally grieve. I'm sorry, this isn't the happiest of topics."

"Don't worry. You can say whatever you need to. That's why I'm here."

"I hardly think you came to San Francisco to attend Mom's funeral, and certainly not to help get me through it. You'll have such lovely memories of your trip to share! I hope you'll at least be able to laugh about them."

"Only with you, I promise."

"You were terrific on the piano. When you said you were a musician, I thought you were just bragging. Everyone in this city claims to be an artist, but I see now I was wrong about you."

"No need for praise. It's actually my job," Thomas replied with a shrug.

"Being able to express your emotions without words must feel like magic."

"But you haven't told me what you do for a living."

"You didn't ask."

"I'm asking now."

"I'm a pastry chef. I'm glad you like my macarons. Eight in a row, that may be a record!"

"A pastry chef?"

"Is that a problem?"

"No, it's just that you're the first pastry chef I've ever met."

"Sorry, I was just messing with you. Actually, I run a bookstore near Union Square. But please, I beg you, don't ask me who my favorite author is. It would ruin everything."

"What do you mean by 'everything'?"

"Our conversation, which already barely makes sense. It is somehow helping me forget why I'm here, though."

Raymond stood by the buffet, looking impatient. Thomas realized it was because of him. He told Manon he was going to get more food and promised to make sure no one came over while he was gone.

He joined his father and filled his plate with a few more macarons, which were somehow slightly less appetizing to him now.

"When you're done flirting—and don't even try to say you're not—maybe the word 'bookstore' will remind you of something?"

"Were you spying on me?"

"I was wandering around, since no one can talk to me. I tried to listen in on Bartel's conversations, but I couldn't bear it. No wonder Camille died. That man could bore the life out of anyone. So, now, '*bookstore*'—does that word bring anything to mind?"

"Books?"

"Excellent. You're on the right track. And when you buy books, what do you put them in to take them home? A bag! And what else can a bag hold? My ashes, which you forgot inside the Columbarium!"

"Oh shit!"

"Oh shit, indeed."

"I'll go get them right now."

"I would have begun by telling you to do just that, but the guard has locked the doors. Hopefully, he'll open them up again this afternoon. In the meantime, you can go back to flirting, now that you've essentially buried your father."

"I 'buried' you five years ago!"

"And you're insolent too. In any case, Operation Urn is turning out to be a disaster."

"'Operation Urn'? Really?"

But Raymond had disappeared, leaving Thomas frowning at the spot where he'd been.

"Who were you talking to?" Manon asked as she approached.

"To myself. Pianists are lonely people."

A friend of Camille's came over and helped herself to a large glass of white wine. She was wearing a large Afro wig dyed in psychedelic colors and winked conspicuously at them as she left.

"I imagine your father's funeral was more conventional than this?"

"As ordinary as an unfinished symphony."

An hour passed, the guests slowly trickling out. When the room was almost empty, Thomas noticed Mr. Bartel sitting on a chair, his gaze lost in the distance.

"I feel like your father might need you," he whispered to Manon.

She looked over at him.

"He couldn't stand visiting her in that home where we locked her up. Or maybe he just couldn't stand the fact that he couldn't keep his wife in their home. My father has always gotten what he wants, all without cheating, lying, or sucking up. Hard work and determination have always been enough to do the trick. At his level of accomplishment, that's not as common as you'd think. His high principles don't exactly make him easy to live with, but I also don't know anyone who's as honest as he is. That said, I could never figure out how my parents fit together. They loved and respected one another, even admired each other, but they were always distant. There was no affection between them, which is absurd—Mom was such a joyful person. She was so full of life that I often wondered what they had in common. Maybe it's like they say—opposites attract. Were your parents happy together?"

"I never understood much about them, either, at least not until very recently. They divorced ten years before my father's death. After their divorce, they got along beautifully. They often had dinner together. Mom enjoyed his company. Dad made her laugh, and she calmed him down."

"I have to admit, I'm jealous. I would have preferred that, and I'm sure my mother would have too. My father is very old-fashioned, though, so divorce wasn't an option. Still, you're right. I should go talk to him." She sighed. "I don't know how to thank you."

"For what? I haven't enjoyed myself this much in a long time . . . I'm referring to playing the piano, of course."

"You're so awkward that it's almost charming," Manon mused with a smile. She kept her eyes on him for a long time and then, after hesitating, suggested they have dinner together the following night. "As friends, of course," she clarified.

Thomas told her that he would be on a plane. He had to go back to Paris and then on to Warsaw, where he would be playing on Saturday night.

"Now I'm *really* jealous," Manon said.

"Do you really dream of sleeping in crummy hotels and waking up in the morning wondering which city you're in?"

"No. But you get to travel the world and share your talents with audiences who are thrilled to hear you."

"If they were always thrilled, I wouldn't have a million butterflies in my stomach every time I go onstage. Classical music audiences have incredibly high standards. I feel like I'm taking a test every time, like the audience members have the score on their laps and are watching the measures carefully, listening for even the slightest mistake. What's keeping you from traveling?"

"My mom did these past few years."

"But now that you're free? My God, you're right . . . my social ineptitude defies belief."

"We could exchange contact information. You never know. Maybe I'll visit Paris sometime, now that I'm *free*," she added mockingly.

They typed their numbers and email addresses into each other's phones.

Manon looked closely at him again. "Are you sure you never lived in San Francisco?" she asked.

"Never. Where did you live in France?"

"In the south, but I was so little that I only have a few memories. The port in Beaulieu, a Greek revival house at the end of a peninsula, a pizzeria near the beach . . . And I'm not even sure if they're real memories or things people told me. We spent our vacations in Brittany to escape the summer heat, but those memories are even fuzzier. I have a vague one of a club where my mom took me for pony riding lessons, and a merry-go-round that I hated because its dead-eyed wooden horses scared me to death, and I almost forgot—"

"A creperie!"

"Yes, exactly! How did you know?"

"Oh, Brittany is known for its creperies, that's all," Thomas replied carefully. "It wasn't much of a stretch."

"I'm terribly talkative, aren't I?"

"There's nothing terrible about it."

"There is, though; I'll be quiet. I'll let you enjoy your last evening in town. You've spent enough time in this depressing place. Have a good trip. I promise I'll call you whenever I decide to travel back to my childhood home."

Raymond was pacing impatiently at the door, his yawns growing increasingly conspicuous. Thomas joined him, and they walked side by side to the Columbarium.

"What a chatterbox!" Raymond exclaimed.

"She didn't want to be alone. Understandable on a day like today, don't you think?"

"Couldn't her father have helped her with that?"

"I'll get the bag and we can go."

"I hope Camille is still on the altar. This is our last chance."

"What if she's not?"

"I'll have to look around the place to find where they put her."

"I could also ask. That might be easier."

"For you *and* for them. That way, when you break into her cabinet to take the urn, they won't have to wonder who did it."

Thomas silently made his way up the steps to the mausoleum.

A police officer standing guard at the door kept him from going in. They chatted for a moment, then Raymond saw his son turn around and come back without the bag.

"What now?"

Thomas explained what he had learned. Someone close to the mayor was being buried that afternoon. And while they were readying the venue, some Dignity Memorial employees had discovered a suspicious package at the foot of the altar. The bomb squad was verifying its contents.

"Well this is definitely the first time I've ever been mistaken for a bomb."

"Don't worry. I'll explain everything."

Raymond raised his hand to stop his son. "Don't try to explain anything as long as the police are crawling all over this place. Those uniformed cowboys would probably arrest you on the spot and put you on the first plane back to France."

"For what? Leaving a cloth bag behind?"

"For bringing your father's remains to the United States. I don't think that's exactly legal."

"You're just bringing this up now?"

"Better late than never. Isn't that what they say?"

"Do you have a Plan C?"

"Not yet. But we'll think of something. Go into town and enjoy yourself. I'll stay here until I know more."

"How exactly do you move around, anyway?"

"Now is not the time!"

"All right, fine," Thomas said. "We'll meet back at the apartment tonight."

14

The head of Dignity Memorial turned up in the reception room, a dismayed expression on his face. At first, Manon thought he was attempting to look grief-stricken, but she quickly realized this was something else. He wanted to talk to her and her father privately, in his office.

Worried, Mr. Bartel followed with his daughter. Bartel was afraid the man was going to ask for more money and was determined to refuse. He'd signed a quote and wouldn't pay a penny more.

The other man's expression grew even more serious as he asked them to sit down. "I don't know how to say this," he announced, his voice shaking. "Nothing like this has ever happened before. We're doing everything we can to find the culprits."

"What culprits?" asked Mr. Bartel.

"Someone broke the seal on your wife and mother's urn," the man said in a disapproving tone.

"I don't understand," Manon said.

"One or more individuals tried to open it, but don't worry—after conducting a detailed inspection, our team has determined that they failed."

"I'm going to need more details," Mr. Bartel demanded. "What individuals? And what team?"

"We gave the urn to our head of cremation, who inspected it with a magnifying glass. The wax seal was broken but still in place, proving that the lid was never fully removed. Someone did try to open it. But that's all they managed to do."

"Oh, is that all?!" shouted Mr. Bartel. "Who was it?"

"We don't know yet, but rest assured, we're investigating quite thoroughly."

"Maybe one of your employees just dropped it by accident," Manon suggested with a generous smile.

"That's impossible!" the manager objected.

"You think it's more likely that someone tried to open it?"

"Well, even if one of my employees was that incompetent—which is highly unlikely—the seal would be in pieces. And, like I said—"

"It's broken, but still in place," Manon finished his sentence.

"Where is my wife now?" Mr. Bartel asked.

"To compensate you for this, we have provided her with one of the best spots in the Columbarium. A beautiful cabinet in the third row from the bottom, across from a window with a view of the park. It's one of the most expensive locations, but we will cover the difference in cost, of course."

"You have twenty-four hours to find the miserable bastards who committed this shameful act!" Mr. Bartel shouted.

"Maybe it was just an accident," Manon insisted. "Who would do something like that? And why? It doesn't make any sense. Plus, Mom's ashes weren't ever left alone, not even for a second."

"We have one lead," the manager continued, ignoring Manon. "One of our gardeners noticed a man lurking around."

"What happened after we left the mausoleum?" Mr. Bartel asked.

"The same thing that happens after every ceremony. As soon as the last guest left, one of our employees came to take Mrs. Bartel to her new home and close the doors. That's when we realized what had happened."

"Who was the last guest to leave?"

The manager shrugged. Manon decided not to mention that she was the last to leave with Thomas. Nor did she reveal that she had found him near her mother's urn. The man who had generously agreed to replace the organist, who had played Debussy and Vivaldi's *Gloria* with such emotion, and who had agreed to be her wingman all afternoon couldn't have done such a thing. Though maybe he wasn't just awkward. Maybe he was also clumsy, and he had knocked the urn over by accident. She imagined how scared he must have been afterward, and this put a smile on her face. Her father noticed her smirk, which only intensified his rage.

"I'm sure it was an accident," Manon said again as she stood up. "You know what they say: There's no crime without a motive. And what would the motive be in this case? Who wants to steal ashes? The idea is absurd!"

"Oh, so you're a detective now?" Mr. Bartel said sarcastically.

"No, but if you hired one, they would come to the same conclusion. Now, if you'll excuse me, I'm going to pay my respects to what's left of my mother for the last time today, and then I'm going to get some fresh air. Don't get too worked up, Dad. I'll come over for dinner tonight. Now, where is this gorgeous space with the park view?" she said, her tone slightly mocking.

The Dignity Memorial manager called his assistant and asked him to take Ms. Bartel to her mother.

The man led her there in perfect silence and left without a word.

Manon found it soothing to look out her mother's window.

"Alone at last. It's strange, Mom, but I feel like you're still here. The last few months, you didn't say much more than you can now. I really hope you're finally free. Free to go where you want, maybe even farther, as long as you come back to me every now and again. I'd give everything I have for you to hear me. My pianist knocked over your urn. Was that a little sign for me? Another one of your pranks, to let me know you're yourself again? In any case, it looks like it worked out all right for you. This view really is nice."

Mr. Bartel waited in the manager's office for the gardener to arrive and explain what he'd seen. The man's statement wasn't particularly helpful. Early that morning, a man in his thirties, dressed in a black suit, had gone for a walk in the park and sat down on a bench. The gardener had thought it looked like he was talking to himself. Nothing too unusual, though, given their location. A little later, a young woman had come to fetch him.

"What do you mean, 'fetch him'?" Mr. Bartel asked.

"They headed to the mausoleum together, just before the funeral began," the gardener said.

"You need to find that man," Mr. Bartel ordered.

"Sitting on a bench isn't exactly a crime," the manager ventured. "And this man seemed to be one of your guests."

"None of our guests fit that description, but I'll double-check the list as soon as I get home. I'll expect answers from you tomorrow at the latest."

Mr. Bartel left the office without saying goodbye to the manager or his assistant, or to the gardener. But he came back just minutes later with a new request.

Thomas had been unable to resist the urge to return to Davies Symphony Hall. He stopped for a moment on the steps, daydreaming of someday seeing crowds fight their way in to see him play. Then he headed toward Union Square, a large plaza bordered by fancy boutiques, art galleries, souvenir shops, and beauty salons—an oasis of luxury located just steps from O'Farrell Street, where homeless people slept on the sidewalk.

Thomas studied the column that stood in the center of the square. A Greek deity, balancing on one foot, pointed a trident toward the sky.

"It's Nike, the goddess of victory," Raymond explained, appearing suddenly, without warning.

Thomas jumped and turned toward his father, letting out a sigh.

"Did I scare you?"

"What do you think? How do you do that?"

"Simple enough: She's easily recognizable, and she was considered quite a looker in her time. Remarkable balance too!"

"I meant your sudden appearances!"

"No idea. Do I ask you how *you* walk? Everyone has their own way. I come and go as I please," Raymond said. "She was erected to commemorate Admiral Dewey's victory against the Spanish at the Battle of Manila Bay. One of the tines on the trident represents President McKinley, who was assassinated six months after the monument went up. When Roosevelt took office, he dedicated the tine to his predecessor. The irrefutable historical conclusion is that McKinley was considered much sharper after his death than he ever was in life."

"I didn't know you were so familiar with San Francisco," Thomas said, surprised.

"Everything I just told you is explained at the foot of the monument. Humanity has such strange ideas about how to make sure a person is remembered. A statue. So sad."

"Not everyone has the chance to come back and see their son."

"You're right. I'm lucky. Anyway, now that you're done playing tourist, let's sit on those steps over there. We need to talk."

Thomas followed his father and sat down next to a man playing guitar.

"They confiscated my urn!" he told Thomas. "The manager of Dignity Memorial was outraged to learn someone had left a loved one like that. Listening to him go on and on, I felt like a small child who'd been abandoned on the steps of a church. His assistant defended you, suggesting that people of limited means couldn't afford the kind of resting place their loved ones deserved and were no doubt simply counting on the kindness of Dignity and its employees. The manager replied that the person in question could hardly have cremated the body in their fireplace! It was so humiliating. In the meantime, he has me under lock and key in his office. A surgeon of my stature hidden away in a cabinet! What did I ever do to deserve this?"

"I suppose you'll have to take that question up with God."

"I already told you to leave God out of this, and to not go calling him whenever the mood strikes. I said earlier that this was a disaster, but now it's a full-on catastrophe."

"The good news is that we've found your ashes. I'll get them back tomorrow. This isn't anything we can't fix."

"Now it's my turn to ask what planet you live on! What are you going to tell him? That you came here on vacation with your father's remains without a single legal document allowing it? And how do you expect to prove the urn is yours? Or, rather, mine. Are you planning to ask them to take your word for it? You know how they treat foreigners here ever since they elected that yellow-haired mafioso, don't you? If you're lucky, they'll just deport you. If not, they'll link you to the incident with Camille's urn and throw you in jail."

"What incident?"

"Apparently, you didn't close the lid properly after your failed attempt to open it. I didn't know there was a seal. It was still in place but broken, so they noticed it had been tampered with. I guess we can't all be Arsène Lupin!"

Thomas's eyes widened, and his father was surprised to see him blush.

"Does her daughter know?" he asked worriedly.

"Probably. By the way, what color are her eyes?" Raymond asked.

"Topaz blue," Thomas replied. "Why?"

"Topaz blue, right. And you expect me to believe you've forgotten her name!"

"I haven't forgotten it. I don't see what you're getting at."

"I'm your father, but I was your age once, and if you didn't have a thing for her, you wouldn't have paid her so much attention. She's become the apple of your eye. Topaz blue! Speaking of apples, they don't fall far from the tree, son, even when they try to roll as far away as they can."

"Even dead you're full of it. I happened to notice the color of her eyes because I spent a couple hours with her while doing *you* a favor, if you'll recall."

"Really?"

Next to them on the steps, the guitarist started playing Dylan's "I Shall Be Released." Raymond assured his son that he had nothing to do with it.

"All right, I take full responsibility for my mistake, and I promise I'll fix it. I'll go back to the Columbarium tonight and find a way into that office. I'll break into the cabinet and take you back to Paris."

"It's too dangerous, Thomas. I can't let you do that. I made a mistake dragging you into all this. It's over now. Besides, I don't want to go back to your mother's apartment. I'm too old for that. If I'm lucky, maybe they'll put me somewhere near Camille. Worst-case scenario, they'll scatter my ashes outside. This park is still better than the dusty bookcase where I've spent the last five years."

"It's not like I'd be killing anyone."

"Don't be flippant about this! You'd be breaking into a hallowed building. If you got caught, you'd be totally unable to justify your actions or play the sympathy card with a judge. I'd simply hoped that, by bringing you to San Francisco, I might somehow help you realize your dream of playing on an American stage. I don't want both of us to end up locked away."

The guitarist couldn't handle the weirdo talking to himself anymore. He picked up his stuff and found a new spot, farther away.

Thomas fell silent again and watched a tourist couple walk past hand in hand.

"This trip wasn't a mistake," he said.

"You have your whole life ahead of you, son. I refuse to let you take this risk."

"And I refuse to leave you here. What will I tell your grandchildren someday? That I abandoned their grandfather when he needed me?"

"I had no idea you were expecting. Congratulations."

"You act like such a child sometimes."

"Maybe, but I won your mother's heart with my nonsense. Don't ever pass up a chance to make a good joke, especially when you're in dire circumstances."

"Is the office on the ground floor, at least?" asked Thomas.

"Ground floor, third window, first building on the left. I realize fighting you on this is hopeless," Raymond replied innocently.

"We'll go in after midnight, then."

Raymond put his arm around his son's shoulder. "You're right, this trip wasn't a mistake. But I want you to promise me something."

"Tell me what it is, and we'll see."

"Promise me that you'll come back to San Francisco someday and play at Davies Symphony Hall and that, at the end of the concert, as the crowd showers you with applause, you'll think of your father."

"I think of you every time I go onstage."

Raymond was quiet for a moment.

"We should have spent more time together," he said. "Become best friends. I wanted to be a role model for you, to mold you in my image, pass down my values, and I thought doing all that took distance. I felt I'd led an exemplary life; I was a proud man. But everything you've accomplished goes beyond my wildest dreams. I never told you enough just how proud I was of you. Not only of the man you have become, but of the child you were too. Of your determination, your courage, the way you looked out for others. Of that light in your eyes that made me feel like anything was possible."

"Stop it, Dad."

"To hell with modesty. It only keeps us from hearing the things that really matter. I don't have much time; I can feel myself fading little by little. So, I want you to listen to me and make me that promise."

Thomas looked straight into his father's eyes and promised.

15

Thomas walked quickly through Union Square, making his way toward the shops just below the plaza.

"Where are we going?" Raymond asked.

"To buy me a new outfit," Thomas replied.

"In a sportswear store?"

"I think dark, comfortable clothes will be better suited to breaking and entering."

"Arsène managed all right in his suit," Raymond protested.

After a quick stop at the Green Street apartment, where Thomas changed, they arranged to be dropped off six blocks from the Columbarium. Raymond argued that getting any closer would arouse suspicion once people heard about the crime—a theory he'd picked up from a TV show. They waited for the car to drive off before setting out. Raymond stopped short at the intersection of Geary Boulevard and Beaumont Avenue, outside Mel's Drive-In.

"A real drive-in diner!" he exclaimed, his voice filled with childlike glee as he marveled at the blue neon sign. "It's just like the ones in 1950s movies. Come on. It's a bad idea to attempt your mission on an empty stomach. You could faint!"

Thomas looked at his watch. It wasn't yet midnight. Despite his joking tone, his father wasn't completely wrong.

He opened the door to the diner and saw that not a single detail had been missed. A row of green pleather booths ran along the window. Matching chairs clustered around Formica tables, and taller chairs lined up along the counter. A brightly colored jukebox stood at the far end of the room.

"Come look at this!" Raymond shouted. "Your mom and I used to love to dance to 'Rock Around the Clock'! Do you have any change?"

Thomas fumbled in his pocket and pulled out a quarter, which he deposited in the machine. The Bill Haley song filled the room, and the customers sitting at the counter turned briefly to look at him, amused. Raymond and his son sat down at a booth. A waitress wearing a pink top and white apron brought Thomas his meal and a cup of coffee.

"I feel like I'm twenty-five again," Raymond mused as he stroked the seat beneath him.

"Did you go to diners much?"

"I went to the movies every Thursday night and spent the whole time dreaming of having dinner in a place like this. When I left the theater with my friends, we'd walk the streets like we owned them—we thought we were stars. The world was ours for the taking. You can't imagine how happy it makes me to be here. It's the first time I've ever seen one not on the silver screen."

Thomas studied his father's face and decided he looked even younger. Was it because he'd finally realized a lifelong dream? Or was he really rocking backward around the clock?

When they reached the gates to the park just after midnight, Thomas realized that they were much taller than he remembered. The vertical bars offered no holds for his feet. He couldn't grip the points at the top without risking serious injury, either.

"If only I could give you a boost," Raymond grumbled. "It's maddening."

"I wouldn't complain if I were you," Thomas said. "But I'm not sure how we can get around this."

He walked over to one of the two stone columns that flanked the gates and noticed some crevices.

"This could work," he said as he began climbing.

"Don't go breaking your neck," his father warned, then went to wait inside the park.

Thomas jumped down onto the wet grass, and they headed toward the administrative buildings. Raymond led the way, on the lookout for a guard. Thomas followed.

"Are you sure this is the right window?"

"As sure as I am that I'm your father, and the resemblance is undeniable."

Thomas searched the flower bed for a rock large enough to break the window. "Let's hope there's not an alarm."

Raymond gestured at him to stop. "Wait! I hear something. Go hide. I'll find out what's going on."

The only comfortable place Thomas could hide was behind the bench in the middle of the open lawn, which he'd have to cross without any cover, and the quarter moon shone brightly enough to betray any shadow in the park. His only other option was to lie down between two beds of rosebushes. He bit his tongue to keep from crying out as the thorns cut his ankles and forearms.

"All clear, false alarm. I must have dreamt it. Or maybe it was just a rodent," Raymond announced happily. "It's crazy how well I can hear now. Almost too well. Hey, where are you?"

"Here," Thomas groaned as he got to his feet.

"What are you doing on the ground?"

"My hands are bleeding. Less than ideal for my concert!"

Raymond glanced at the wounds and rolled his eyes.

"Just a few tiny scratches. You're such a baby!"

"Did you at least check to see if there's an alarm?" Thomas asked, rubbing his wrists.

"I'll go find out. But only because you asked so nicely."

Raymond walked along the building toward the main door until Thomas coughed, as if urging him to stop. He looked at his son in confusion for a moment, then realized what he wanted.

"Of course! Why do things the hard way?"

He came back and walked through the wall as if it were the most natural thing in the world.

Thomas waited impatiently. A few moments later, his father appeared at the window.

"Nice night, huh?" he said dreamily, looking up at the sky.

"Could you, I don't know, maybe try to concentrate while I'm risking my life for you?"

"I'm trying to lighten the mood. You're so grumpy! Anyway, I'm no expert, but I inspected everything carefully and I didn't find an alarm. No contact monitors on the windows or doors, and no motion detectors."

"You seem to know a lot about the subject."

"I had an alarm installed at your mother's place after I left. Toward the end of our marriage, I wasn't good for much, but I did manage to make her feel safe. The technician who installed it explained everything we might need to know and more. So, are you going to break the window or not?"

After one throw of a stone, the sound of shattered glass, the opening of a window, and a single graceful leap, Thomas finally landed in the Dignity Memorial office.

"Is it in this cabinet?" he asked, pointing toward a corner near the door.

"Yes, I'm crammed between a pile of bills and a mountain of brochures. And they dare call themselves 'Dignity Memorial'!"

Thomas waited for his eyes to adjust to the dark, then got to work. He grabbed a solid-silver letter opener off the desk and pried open the lock. The door swung open, almost falling off its hinges.

"That wasn't exactly discreet. The manager will know precisely what happened when he comes in tomorrow morning."

"I think the broken window will provide him with his first clue," Thomas replied coolly.

He found the urn on one of the shelves and breathed a sigh of relief.

"You're a strange one. You seem happier to see my ashes than you were to see me when I appeared in the office at your mom's place."

"Make jokes all you want, but I wasn't kidding when I said I wouldn't abandon you here."

"It was a poor joke. People make those sometimes when they can't find the words to say what they really feel."

Thomas picked up the rock off the rug.

"Should we kill two birds with one stone?" he asked thoughtfully. "I mean, I've already taken the risk. So, why not go find Camille's urn and complete the mission?"

Raymond floated over to the window and looked out toward the mausoleum.

"Because she's not here anymore." He sighed. "I could feel it as soon as we arrived. That's why I've been a little on edge. I'm sorry."

"Where is she?" Thomas asked.

"I don't know. Her husband must have suspected something. You look so much like me; maybe that got him thinking. That stubborn man has beaten me at every turn. He separated Camille and me once, and now he's kidnapped her. He may have even scattered her ashes already. In any case, there's nothing we can do. Let's go. Tomorrow, you can take me to the beach, and we'll say goodbye one last time. I don't want to go back to Paris. I'd rather stay here, with the ocean air, where Camille lived. You understand that, don't you?"

"And what about me? Where will I go to pay my respects when I need to talk to you? Who will I ask advice from when you're gone?"

"I've been gone for five years, Thomas. You've done quite well without me. We'll find each other in your music. One day, you'll play for a woman, and you'll turn to her for advice. And then you'll play for your children. That's life—I have to go so you can have your turn."

Raymond stepped away from the window to hug his son tightly, their arms intersecting slightly.

"Go on, dry your eyes, son. Let's not waste the hours we have left together. We've had a good time, time we wouldn't have dared to hope we'd get. I traveled the world from conference to conference in my life," he said. "But the best journey I ever took was being your father."

16

Manon had parked along the sidewalk on Sea Cliff Avenue, which wound its way through one of the city's most beautiful neighborhoods. The massive homes and their luxurious yards rivaled one another in size, each one offering a view of Baker Beach and the ocean.

The housekeeper greeted her at the door and took her to the dining room, where her father was waiting in his robe.

"I see you dressed up for me," she quipped.

"I hope you don't mind. I didn't feel up to it tonight. But I'm still happy to see you," he replied softly.

He invited Manon to sit down at the table. Dinner had been ready for half an hour, he said, and the cook had already come out twice to ask when she could serve.

Manon got up immediately to go see her. Teresa had been working for the Bartels for as long as she could remember. Having grown up with her always around, Manon thought of Teresa as a fully-fledged member of the family.

"I hope he's not giving you a hard time," Manon whispered as she hugged the cook.

"He's the one having a hard time at the moment, dear. He's as strong-willed as ever, but he's not fooling me. And you're late, as usual."

"It was a long day."

"I know," Teresa sighed, "but it's over now. You won't have to spend your afternoons in that terrible place anymore. Your mother is better off where she is now."

"If she's anywhere," Manon replied.

"Oh, she's definitely somewhere!"

"Do you have a private line to the great beyond?" Manon asked teasingly.

"Not to the great beyond, but I see everything that goes on in this house."

"Maybe I'm just too tired to get it, but I don't understand what you're saying."

"I'm not saying anything, since I'm not allowed," the cook answered as she carefully poured the contents of a pot into a porcelain tureen. "But I don't approve."

"Of what?"

"Nothing! My lips are sealed. Strict orders from management." This was what she called Mr. Bartel whenever he was getting on her nerves.

"What orders?" Manon pressed.

"Go to the table. I didn't spend all that time in the kitchen for you to eat your dinner cold. Think of the poor flounder I keep taking out of the oven only to have to put it back again—he'll get dizzy. After dinner, you can do whatever you like. For example, maybe you'd like to go to the library. It's up to you."

"All right, then. I'll go now."

"You will not!" Teresa cried as she grabbed Manon's arm. "You would have made a terrible spy. Get out of here! Leave my kitchen and go sit with your father."

Teresa gave her a stern look, like she used to when Manon was a child. Even as an adult, Manon didn't dare disobey her orders. Her father himself only risked it on occasion.

Manon sat down across from her father and waited for Teresa to serve the pea soup.

"You should redecorate this room. The wallpaper and wainscoting are depressing." She looked up at the portrait of General Sherman hanging above the mantel. It had frightened her since childhood. "He's been giving me dirty looks for nearly thirty years! Couldn't you find a more cheerful painting? And you never open the curtains. What's the point of living in such a fancy neighborhood if you never see what's going on outside?"

"You can do what you like with your apartment. Just leave me and my house be. Who was the organist you hired for the ceremony?" her father asked.

"An organist," Manon answered dryly.

"Does he have a name?"

"He must, but I don't know it. Why?"

"He seemed to be having a good time. Such enthusiasm and passion. Your mother's friends really enjoyed it."

"That's how she would have wanted it, don't you think?"

"Maybe, but it seemed a bit much to me. You really don't know who he is?"

"Should I?"

"You must have found him somewhere. I asked the head of Dignity Memorial, and he told me you took care of the music."

"That's not true. I went through them."

"At first, but their musician was unable to perform because of an accident this morning. But you already knew that, since you're the one who fixed the problem."

"Why are you so interested in this man?"

"It's not every day that a man buries his wife. And you know very well my passion for details. I just want to know who he is. Especially since you spent the whole reception chatting with him and avoiding all our friends. It was very rude."

"A daughter doesn't bury her mother every day, either. I was tired of being polite and fielding condolences. If you must know, I asked him not to leave my side so people would steer clear. He did exactly as I asked, and I don't care what our friends thought."

"It's strange he didn't tell you his name, though."

"I didn't ask!"

"That's even stranger."

"What are you getting at?"

"You haven't answered my question. The musician didn't just fall from the sky, so where did you find him?"

"On a bench in the park, where I found him humming perfectly in tune with a nice voice, so I took a chance and got lucky. Happy now?"

Manon's father gave her a distressed look.

"Will you spend more time at the bookstore now?" he asked after a moment.

"Will you spend less time at your office now?"

"Don't talk to me like that. You should open a second location in another neighborhood, think about growing your business."

"I didn't get into bookselling to make money. I did it because I enjoy the company of books. Speaking of which, I'd like to borrow one."

Manon pushed her chair back and left her father alone at the dining room table. Since the beginning of the meal, she hadn't stopped thinking about what Teresa could have been hinting at. But she understood immediately when she opened the door to the library.

The urn containing her mother's ashes was sitting on the grand piano.

Manon walked over without speaking. Her father broke the silence when he came in after her.

"She loved music so much, this seemed the best place for her. Don't you think?"

"What is Mom doing here?" Manon cried. "Won't you ever let her be?"

"After what happened at the Columbarium, I wanted to protect her."

Manon abruptly decided to change tactics. She went to her father and took his hands in hers. "Dad, you know that's not why. Mom couldn't be in this house anymore; it wasn't your fault. Stop torturing yourself. I know you like the back of my hand. You've always prided yourself on being able to handle anything, but you couldn't have prevented her disease from getting worse. No one could've."

"I never visited her. I couldn't stand it when she didn't recognize me. I don't understand why I was so weak, but I just couldn't do it. I would take the car and drive all the way there, only to turn around when I got to her door. I never even got a chance to say I was sorry. So, when I came home earlier, I sat down on the bench and—"

"She forgave you long before she died," Manon reassured her father, whose red eyes were brimming with tears. "She didn't want you to see her there. She said she preferred it that way. She didn't want you to have that memory of her. She even said she was selfish to want to keep you away."

"Did she really say that?" her father asked.

Manon nodded, confirming her little white lie.

"Let me take her back to her final resting place at the Columbarium," she urged.

Her father placed his hand on the urn. "Not right away. Can't we leave her here for a little while? For just a few days?"

"Just a few days," Manon repeated.

Neither of them felt like returning to dinner. Teresa had gathered as much from eavesdropping on the beginning of their conversation and had since cleared the table and brought herbal tea to the library for the two of them.

Manon sat down on the couch, her father in the armchair.

"Which book?" he asked.

"I'm sorry?"

"You wanted to borrow one."

Manon got up and pretended to look for a title on the shelves.

"It's funny, sometimes you're an amazing liar, and other times you're so bad it's painful." Her father's vulnerability had lasted only minutes. "I'll have to have a chat with Teresa tomorrow morning."

"Don't you dare scold her. She had your best interests at heart."

"I think I know better than anyone else what's in my best interest."

Manon studied the urn, which shone in the lamplight. "Mom has spent enough time locked up inside," she said decisively. "I'll come back tomorrow, and we'll go scatter her ashes on the beach. That's what she would have wanted. To be free at last."

"How do you know what she would have wanted? Your mother didn't bother to take the time to write a will. I had to learn from one of her friends that she wanted to be cremated and from you that she wanted that burlesque funeral I reluctantly agreed to."

"You're impossible. Stop criticizing her. Mom couldn't have known what would happen to her. You love to be in control so much; what would you do if you realized you were losing control of yourself? She was dignified until the end, and that's worth more than a will, don't you think?"

"I refuse to let her go," her father said.

"She's already gone, whether you like it or not. A man can't own a woman—not even you."

"That's enough. I don't want to fight. It's been a hard day for both of us. Go home. I'll walk you to your car. We'll talk about all this tomorrow, after a good night's sleep."

Manon let her father accompany her to her Prius.

"Another one for your collection," he said as he pulled a parking ticket off the windshield.

Manon took it from him and sat down behind the wheel.

He bent down next to the window. "I'm sure your organist is behind this whole thing."

"What thing?"

"You know what I'm talking about. I want to know how you met him."

"You're ridiculous. He was walking through the mausoleum garden yesterday, and I ran into him. During our short conversation, he mentioned he was a musician. When I saw him again this morning, I'd just found out that the organist I had hired was unable to perform. He was a gentleman and agreed to do me a huge favor. Mom's urn must have been bumped by a clumsy employee. It was an accident, that's all."

"But what was this gentleman doing on the grounds of the mausoleum two days in a row?"

"Do you really think you're the only person who's ever lost someone? But sure, he must have come all the way from Paris to open Mom's urn."

"What do you mean, 'from Paris'?" Her father looked intrigued.

"He's French. Can I go now?"

Manon said good night to her father and closed the window, then started the car.

Mr. Bartel watched the Prius drive off into the distance. When he went back inside, he placed Camille's urn in the library closet and set an alarm before going to bed.

Raymond was watching TV in the living room. Thomas was dozing in the bedroom. *Ray Donovan* was on Showtime.

"*Rway* is pretty good, don't you think?" said Raymond, struggling to pronounce the name with an American accent.

"What are you talking about?" his son mumbled.

"Maybe I'll start going by Ray for short! So stylish."

"How are you still so obsessed with style at your age?" asked Thomas.

"What do you mean? I'm ageless!"

Thomas sat up in bed. His father was trying to act lighthearted, but he wasn't fooled. Yes, he'd managed to get Raymond's urn back. But their trip was still a failure.

He got up and grabbed his laptop, and when he checked his email, he found one from Manon.

Dear Thomas,

When I got home earlier, I turned on my computer to catch up on all the work I haven't kept up with these past few months. I don't remember if I told you, but I run a bookstore on Geary Street. It's not very big, but I love it. My mind was wandering, so I did a little digging online. I know it's very nosy of me, but it's to be expected in this day and age. I typed in the words "pianist" and "France" and found out who you are. When I saw the videos of you performing, I realized what an amazing gift you gave me today. How many people came to see you play in Stockholm? A thousand? Two thousand? Maybe more.

I feel terrible about making you play for fifty people—and in a mausoleum! You didn't ask for anything in return, despite the fact that I was a perfect stranger and the repertoire was hardly the one you're used to. I just needed to write to thank you and to let you know I'll always remember what you did for me.

I love the company of books and wouldn't change professions for the world, but the look in your eyes when you were playing was something I've never seen before. I'll admit, I envied you.

If I make it to France someday, I'll come hear you play. I imagine that, given all the faces you must see on your tours, you'll have forgotten mine by then, but

I'll remind you of the day I buried my mother, when you helped comfort a stranger.

Thank you for being there and for your generosity.
Manon

Thomas read through the email a second time before drafting his own.

Dear Manon,

I'm not the disinterested Samaritan you think I am.

I knew perfectly well who you were. The truth is unbelievable. If only I'd been able to share this part of it with you sooner.

My father and your mother were madly in love for over twenty years. They loved one another in silence, despite the physical distance between them and the obligations and expectations of the time. I only found out recently, while learning about my father's last wishes.

I lied to you. I didn't just happen to be in that park. I had come to steal your mother's remains on the very day you were burying her, in order to fulfill their ultimate wish—to be together forever.

I'd like to find the words to justify my actions, but there aren't any.

You don't owe me any thanks. In fact, I owe you an apology.

Please know that I only acted out of love for my father. I guess I decided eternity was worth a lie.

Please forgive me.
Thomas

The television had just gone silent. Thomas quickly closed his computer before he could send the email. He slipped it under the covers and buried his head in his pillow.

Raymond watched his son from the doorway and smiled. "I can't sleep, either. Well, you know what I mean. You can sleep on the plane. I'll spend tonight in the living room. Try to get some rest."

Thomas didn't answer. Raymond left after telling him he would hurt his eyes by squeezing them shut so tightly.

Thomas waited until all was still and quiet, then got up to put away his computer. When he opened his suitcase, he found the wooden box he'd taken from his mother's house along with his father's ashes. He stared at it for a few moments, then went to the bathroom for his nail clippers.

He carefully forced the lock and got back into bed to begin reading.

At two o'clock in the morning, Thomas returned Camille's last letter to its envelope. As he slipped it back into the box, he felt there was still a sliver of hope.

All wasn't lost just yet.

17

Detective Pilguez parked his Ford station wagon in the Columbarium visitors' lot. As he made his way up the path to the administrative building, he shuddered.

The manager's assistant welcomed him at the door with a scowl that rivaled his own, then took him to his boss's office, where the executive seemed even more disturbed than either of them were.

"There you are, finally! They broke the window and forced the cabinet door open," he moaned.

"I can see perfectly well, thanks. Nice cabinet, by the way. Did they close it before they left, or did you cover the crime scene in your greasy fingerprints so you could make my job even harder?"

With that, the detective set the tone. The manager stuttered as the officer began to draw his own conclusions about what had occurred.

"What kind of valuables were inside? Money? Bonds?"

"Just files."

"Incriminating ones, I imagine, for someone to take the time to burgle such a depressing place."

"They didn't take any papers. Just an urn."

"A what?" Pilguez frowned.

"A funerary urn."

"Ah, and nothing else?"

"That's quite a lot already."

"If you say so. Was it made of gold?"

"Brass. The urn itself has no real value."

"What was inside, then?"

"Ashes, of course."

"Ah," repeated Pilguez.

"Don't you understand? They stole human remains. This is very serious."

"Whose remains?"

"That's the problem. We have no idea."

"Ah!"

There was an awkward silence.

"I know plenty of people with skeletons in their closets, but this takes the cake. What were the remains doing in your office?"

"Someone had shamefully abandoned them here late yesterday morning. As soon as we found them, we dutifully took them in. We couldn't just leave them lying around."

"So, you took in a lost soul, in a way. I must say your profession seems much more interesting than I would have expected."

"I can hear your sarcasm, detective. I realize this type of case isn't exactly routine, but please do everything you can to find—"

"To find whoever it is," Pilguez grumbled. "Jesus, what on earth did I do to deserve cases like this? So, let me see if I got this right. Someone left an urn in a cemetery—not a totally unreasonable thing to do, when you think about it—"

"Not a *cemetery*, a columbarium," the manager protested in a pinched tone.

"You locked it up, and it escaped during the night," the detective continued, as if the manager hadn't spoken. "Thirty years chasing criminals and now I'm chasing down an urn—so this is what it's come to. Did it ever occur to you that the urn could maybe contain something other than ashes? Drugs, for example?"

"Impossible. We opened it."

"Are you absolutely sure? You didn't . . . No, of course not, that would be unseemly. But if there weren't any drugs inside, why would someone steal something that had been abandoned just hours before?"

"You're the police officer."

"More's the pity! Let's go back to the beginning, then," Pilguez said as he took a notebook and pen out of his jacket pocket. "Any idea when the break-in took place?"

"I left my office at eight o'clock, just before the gates closed. Our night watchman makes rounds in the park, but he didn't notice anything strange. I don't know any more than that."

"Theft of a funerary urn from the manager's office," Pilguez mumbled as he took notes. "What is it worth?"

"It has only sentimental value, I suppose."

"Well, it's going to cost your insurance company a fortune. No surveillance cameras?"

"This is a very nice neighborhood. Our residents are perfectly safe. Or, at least, that's what we thought until last night. We'll have some installed, you can take my word for it."

"Of course. No fingerprints, no video, no identity. Hard to crack a kidnapping case without any leads."

"A kidnapping?" the manager cried. "Do you think they'll ask for a ransom?"

"I wouldn't think so."

"How can you be sure?"

"They can hardly threaten to kill the hostage. As for negotiating the return of the remains, no one even knows who's in there."

The manager nodded and slumped into his chair. "Why, then?"

"That's a good question. I'll admit the motive is unclear. Did anything strange happen yesterday? Even the slightest thing being off could put me on the right track."

The manager stroked his chin and thought hard. "Now that you mention it, our organist had an accident yesterday, and someone replaced him at the last minute."

"Now that's the lead I was missing!" the detective exclaimed, slapping his thigh. "Now I'll be able to solve the case in no time."

"Really?" the manager and his assistant asked in unison.

"No, of course not. All right. What happened to your organist?"

"He slipped in the shower."

"Fascinating! Who replaced him?"

"We don't know that, either. It wasn't anyone who works for us. Actually, while we're on the topic, our gardener saw the very same musician in the park the day before."

"But the urn was left yesterday?"

"Truly, no detail escapes you, detective. Maybe he was casing the place. Mr. Bartel's daughter spoke to him. In fact, she's the one who went and got him for the service. Our gardener saw them together outside."

"Where might I find this young woman?"

"We have her father's address."

The detective copied it down in his notebook and left.

Thomas woke up late. He heard noise coming from the living room and found his father sitting in front of the TV.

"How did you turn it on?"

"No idea. I thought really hard about it and poof! Wavelengths work in mysterious ways—I spent my entire life working as a surgeon only to be reincarnated as a remote control. Totally worth it, am I right?"

Thomas sat down next to him. He wished they could trade places, wished he could protect and reassure his father. He would have liked to tell him that things would be better the next day, even though he knew they were running out of time together. But Raymond made the first move, as always, to console Thomas.

"Don't be glum, son. We tried. And this trip gave us some extra time together. Not everyone gets that. I can't bear to see you sad because of me. I had a wonderful life, and yours will be even better. Think of all that's ahead of you: concerts, love, the beauty of sunrises, the joy of being alive, everything you have yet to experience. It's wonderful. Do you realize how lucky you are? Don't waste a single second feeling sorry for me. I made my choices and wouldn't change them for the world. Even though I worked a lot, I raised you too; I loved you, watched you grow and become a man—such a good man! So, believe me, I'll be going without any regrets, except for Camille, but I'm sure she'll understand. You and I don't have much time left, so go ahead, ask me anything you want. Actually, just ask me one question, whichever one is most important to you, and I promise to answer."

Thomas looked affectionately at his father and asked, "Tell me, Dad: What does it mean to be a father?"

"What time is your plane?"

Manon lifted the metal security gate halfway up and ducked to get into the bookstore. Then she turned off the alarm and looked around. She loved this time of day, before opening, when she could walk alone among the shelves, take inventory of her stock, flip through a book she grabbed off a table, or choose what she would read to her mother in the afternoon. She put down the book she'd picked up. It struck her that, starting now, life was back to normal. Manon wasn't the kind of person to let herself wallow; she had inherited Camille's optimism.

She walked into the storeroom and started opening boxes full of the summer's new releases. Books were published seasonally, but their release dates didn't always coincide with the best time for reading them. Manon spent a lot of time shelving them appropriately. She would place them on tables, arranging them like flowers in a vase—never by theme. She wanted to kindle customers' curiosity. Booksellers live to answer readers' questions. Giving advice, making recommendations, and sharing in a customer's delight all brought her joy, even when the reader wasn't particularly friendly.

That thought reminded her of the order she had placed for the antiques dealer next door. She rifled through the boxes she'd received that week and pulled out the titles he'd requested. Then she returned to her desk behind the counter to start on the accounting. A pile of bills was waiting—but they would have to wait some more.

She had just received a text.

Saying that he needed time to pack, Thomas escaped to the bedroom while his father watched yet another episode of his new favorite show. He climbed out the window, crossed the yard, walked up the alley that ran along the side of the house, and knocked on his hosts' door.

A few minutes later, he returned the way he'd come.

Next, he worked up the courage to call his agent and ask for a favor.

"What are you doing in San Francisco?" Marie-Dominique asked. "I believe you're supposed to be in Paris."

"My father always said belief is for religion."

"Leave your poor father out of it. So, what's your plan exactly? Are you going to come back to Paris—in time to hop on a plane to Warsaw and play after flying all night? Is that really reasonable?"

"More reasonable than canceling the concert. But I have no choice. I have to stay here one more day."

"So, you need me to get your ticket to Warsaw." Marie-Dominique sighed. "Will you ever change?"

"If I changed, you wouldn't like me as much."

"Who says I like you? You're terrible."

"Marie-Do, don't make me beg. Oh, all right, I'm begging you."

"A simple 'please' would have done the trick. Fine, I'll get you a San Francisco–Warsaw flight. I can't promise it'll be direct, but I'll make sure you get there on time. And you, you'd better play like a god, jet lag be damned."

"Don't I always?"

"Arrogant to boot! I hear you slipped up at Pleyel last Friday. The conductor was not pleased."

"Bad workmen blame their tools. If he had done a better job conducting, he wouldn't have had anything to complain about."

"Right, it's his fault. Of course. Well, since I'm now apparently a travel agent as well as your music agent, I will take care of your problem and then get back to work. I'll send you an email with the details. Don't miss that plane, Thomas. Warsaw is expecting you, and the concert is fully booked."

Thomas promised and hung up. He kept his phone in his hand to type a message, which he sent just before going back in to see his father.

Manon looked at her phone and smiled as she reread the message.

I missed my plane. Is your invitation to dinner still open?

How did you manage that?

It doesn't take off until this afternoon.

How do you know that?

I have a gift.

So do I. Mine's missing planes that haven't left yet.

Okay.

???

Okay to dinner!

Where would you like to go?

Pick me up at the bookstore at 7.

On Geary Boulevard?

Good memory. See you later.

Thomas put his phone away and walked into the living room.

"Are you ready?" his father asked.

"I'm not leaving."

"What are you talking about?"

"You're still here. I'll stay with you until the end. That's what it means to be a son."

Raymond turned around and smiled. "I'm so glad to have one."

Then he returned to his episode.

Pilguez arrived at Mr. Bartel's home around noon. His long career had taught him to pay special attention to the way people reacted when they first saw his badge. Surprise, distrust, or goodwill—each one said a lot. Mr. Bartel's reaction, however, didn't fit any of these categories. In fact, he seemed to have been waiting for the detective. It was almost like he was relieved.

"Ah, so they've decided to file charges. I was just about to do it myself."

"Is the urn yours?"

"Of course, it's my wife's."

"Do you know where it is?"

"In the library."

"With Colonel Mustard?"

"Excuse me?"

"If the urn contains your wife's ashes, why did you steal it?"

"I didn't steal anything at all. What are you talking about? The manager of the Columbarium knows very well why I couldn't let him keep her."

"I've come straight from his office, and he didn't seem to be in the know."

Pilguez studied his surroundings. Wainscoting, crown moldings, fine oak detailing, antique furniture, paintings by master artists on the walls—luxury in all its forms. It occurred to him that his entire salary wouldn't be enough to purchase the pair of wing chairs in front of him.

"Something doesn't make sense. A man of your circumstances would have called his lawyers instead of breaking a window. What came over you?"

"I don't understand a single thing you're saying. Someone tried to open my wife's urn after the funeral. I assumed it was the work of an unstable person and asked Dignity Memorial to give it back to me to prevent him from doing it again. I signed a form and brought Camille back home."

"Your deceased wife, I assume."

"What window are you talking about?"

Pilguez didn't answer. Instead, he asked Mr. Bartel if his daughter was in.

"Manon? What does she have to do with any of this?"

"Your wife isn't the only one to have left the Columbarium. An urn was stolen last night, and the only lead I have—if it's even a lead at all, I have my doubts about that—is a gardener's claim that he saw a suspicious man in the park with your daughter."

"Come in," Bartel ordered. "I might know who he is."

Pilguez followed Mr. Bartel to his office. The splendor of the first room was nothing compared to the ostentatious luxury he found in this one. A Louis XVI desk with matching marquise chairs, Persian rugs—even the wallpaper and curtains looked priceless. The detective gawked at a Picasso and a van Gogh.

"Do you like art?" Bartel asked.

"I do when it's in a museum. Might I ask what you do for a living?"

"If you think it will help with your investigation."

"No, I'm just curious. You said you knew the suspect?"

"I said I think I might know who he is. That's not exactly the same thing. But before I say more, I need to know you'll leave my daughter out of all this."

"I promise to do my job. We'll see about the rest."

The two men sized each other up, then Bartel turned his computer screen around.

"Are you going to a concert tonight?" Pilguez asked as he studied the poster on the screen.

"This is your criminal."

Pilguez leaned in and examined the features of the pianist posing in front of a grand piano at Stockholm's opera house.

"What makes you so sure? Sweden isn't exactly next door."

"He was there yesterday, at the Columbarium. I recognize him."

"But, just moments ago, you corrected me, saying you didn't know him. So, how did you identify this person as Thomas Saurel?"

"By looking up 'pianist,' 'French,' and 'concerts.' It's not rocket science. I'll be sure to donate some money to your precinct so you can replace your typewriters with computers," Bartel joked bitterly.

Pilguez stared at the bereaved man, a fiery look in his eyes. "You're arrogant, just like every other person who's never had to struggle. But your show of money doesn't impress me. You couldn't pay me to spend a single night in this house. You'd better change your tone if you want this conversation to continue."

Bartel looked at his feet and, after a brief silence, apologized, blaming his behavior on the pain of having lost his wife.

"Who told you he was French?" Pilguez asked as he sat down on the corner of the desk.

"Manon."

"So, she knows him well, then?"

"No," Bartel protested. "She met him the day before yesterday at the mausoleum. They ran into each other, and he told her he was a musician. When she learned yesterday morning that our organist was unable to perform, she asked him to perform in his place."

"And he accepted."

"Just to have an in, I'm sure of it."

"But he could have just walked right in, couldn't he? The Columbarium is open to visitors."

"I mean he wanted to get access to Camille!"

"Maybe, but why would a renowned concert pianist want to open an urn? It's a bit morbid."

"It's more complicated than that. Manon doesn't know most of what I'm about to tell you. And I need it to stay that way."

Pilguez listened patiently as Mr. Bartel told him all about what had brought him to the United States over twenty years earlier.

"All right, so let's imagine this young man wanted to see what his father's mistress looked like. Actually, he was a little late for that, wasn't he? But let's imagine it was him anyway. What you're suggesting is a misdemeanor, but not a serious crime. That still doesn't link him to the robbery case I'm working on."

"Of course it does. That troublemaker wanted to damage my wife's urn, despite the fact that she never even became the mistress of that sneaky surgeon. Since he missed his first chance, he came back at night, found Camille's cabinet empty, guessed the manager had put the urn in a safe place, and broke into his office to find it. Only, the idiot took the wrong urn."

"A postmortem vendetta. It's a bit of a stretch, don't you think? In any case, I don't buy it."

"But it's so obvious. He wanted to succeed where his father had failed by kidnapping my wife!"

"To do what, take her on a date? Be reasonable, Mr. Bartel. I know you're going through a difficult time, but you have to admit that it doesn't make any sense. How old is this man, in his thirties? If he's performing for the Queen of Sweden, he must be doing pretty well as a pianist. Do you really think he'd cross the Atlantic and risk ruining his life just to get revenge for his father? By stealing ashes? I don't know a single prosecutor in town who would agree to file charges against someone with such a crazy motive."

"A man tries to steal my wife, then his son turns up at her funeral. And you think that's a coincidence?" Bartel shouted as he pounded his fist on the desk.

"Your wife was not a Louis XVI desk. And since she followed you here, no one stole her. Besides, all this took place so long ago. Did the son even know your wife?"

"Of course he knew her. Camille and Raymond used our children as an excuse to be together. They met on the sly next to the merry-go-round, by the swings, or at the beach. That's where I caught them."

"But it was so long ago that your daughter didn't even recognize the child she used to play with. Did this boy maintain any sort of relationship with your wife? Did they see each other after you moved?"

Clearly outraged by the question, Bartel loudly replied that that was obviously impossible.

"Let me suggest a slightly more believable version of the facts. Our pianist, in San Francisco—maybe for a concert—learns that your wife's funeral will take place during his stay. If we suppose he knew anything about his parents' love lives—which, need I remind you, your daughter didn't—he decides to attend, out of curiosity. When his childhood friend, who doesn't recognize him, asks him to help out by replacing the organist, he agrees, maybe even to make up for his father's mistakes. All I see is a strange but poetic twist of fate. I'll question him, on principle, but believe me, he's not the culprit."

"I don't know where you'll find him," Bartel replied, now more convinced than ever that his version of the facts was the right one.

"I'll call Immigration Services and have an address by this afternoon."

Pilguez decided he'd wasted enough time. This investigation was going nowhere. Someone had stolen an unknown person's urn, and no one would ever know why. Maybe it was a family matter—some next of kin who didn't want to pay for a final resting place had ditched the deceased's remains and then changed his or her mind, racked with guilt. Or maybe someone else had decided to put the urn back. Either way, the thief had almost certainly scattered the ashes since. The truth of what had happened would forever remain a mystery.

Nevertheless, his professional conscience urged him to call a colleague in Immigration from the car. He asked for a copy of Thomas Saurel's entry record. If the musician was innocent, it would be possible to find him at the address provided. In the meantime, he looked up Manon Bartel online and learned that she was a bookseller.

Pilguez took off toward Geary Boulevard to question her, convinced that she knew much more than she'd told her father.

Manon invited him into the bookstore, seemingly unsurprised by his visit. She obviously knew who had sent him. She offered him her chair and leaned her back against the counter.

"It's small but rather charming, don't you think?" she asked.

"A lot more charming than your father's house, I have to say."

"I was sure he'd send you to question me. I should have put money on it. He's so stubborn."

"You would have lost your bet. In fact, he forbade me to come near you. That piqued my interest, of course."

"He's obsessed with what happened with Mom's urn. It must have been dropped by one of the funeral home employees. They blamed it on a stranger to cover their backs, but their theory is so absurd I don't even know why they bothered contacting the police."

"I got involved by way of a slightly more serious crime."

He told her about the theft that had been committed and Mr. Bartel's accusations of Thomas Saurel. Manon confirmed that she and Thomas had spoken, emphasizing that he had been a real gentleman to agree to do her such a favor, particularly since he was used to playing for sold-out concert halls.

"Can I show you something?" She opened her laptop and clicked on a YouTube video of Thomas at the concert in Stockholm. "Just look at the expression on his face while he plays."

The detective was watching Manon and not the recording. The sound was barely audible, but one glance at the screen was enough to make the pianist's talents clear.

"Now listen to this," she said enthusiastically, turning on the stereo that played ambient music throughout the bookstore. "It's him," she said, and then fell silent.

Liszt's *Consolations* filled the store. Manon turned the volume up again in the middle of the piece.

The detective handed her the box of tissues he'd noticed on the counter. "Here," he said, "you shouldn't listen to this kind of music at a time like this. It's enough to make even me tear up."

"How could you believe that the person who recorded this album is a common grave robber? My dad is like a dog with a bone. Maybe he's just being overprotective because he saw me talking to Thomas?"

"Probably."

"I'm sorry you came here for nothing."

"How well do you know Thomas Saurel?"

"Like I said, we met for the first time the day before yesterday. Why do you ask?"

"No reason."

Manon leaned in toward Pilguez and studied his face. "Are you keeping something from me?"

"Nothing I could reveal to you in good conscience."

"Do you have evidence that incriminates him? No, of course not. You're trying to sow the seeds of doubt to see if I'm hiding anything. I've seen this hundreds of times in cop shows."

"You watch too much television. Talk to your father. He'll tell you more."

"I'd rather talk to you. Come on, spill it."

"Isn't that supposed to be my line?"

"It's good to switch things up every now and then."

"I'll admit, today hasn't exactly been routine . . . Look, Thomas Saurel, this pianist of yours . . . you've known him longer than you think," the detective admitted.

Manon responded with only silence, making Pilguez wonder if Mr. Bartel's accusations were really as baseless as he'd believed. To find out, he offered her a deal. "A secret in exchange for a promise," he proposed.

"What promise?"

"I thought you'd ask what secret. Here it is: Don't tell your father anything I'm about to tell you. I'm not kidding, either. If you rat me out, I promise that your car, which is partly blocking the sidewalk out front, will never again enjoy such leniency. I'll have my colleagues give you so many parking tickets that you'll have to start riding your bike—which isn't exactly easy in this town."

"All right, you've scared me straight. You have my promise. You didn't need to threaten me, by the way. I always keep my word."

As soon as she learned the truth about her mother's past, memories of her childhood began to make their way to the surface. And once they did, Manon finally understood why Thomas's face had seemed so familiar.

18

"My dad told you that my mom fell in love with this doctor?"

"Quite the opposite. He insisted that their brief connection didn't mean a thing. But the fact that he and your mother left everything behind to live on the opposite side of the world leads me to believe that he took her away from someone who was more than just a crush."

"I'm inclined to believe him. Mom never said a thing to me about it, and I was her best friend."

"You were her daughter. I don't know very many parents who would share such a big secret with their children, especially one that involved loving a man who wasn't their father."

At first, Manon was speechless. The detective sat quietly, giving her time to process what she'd just learned. She soon pulled herself together and decided she had no reason to judge. If her mother had had feelings for another man, that was her story to tell or not to tell, and it appeared she'd turned the page and left that chapter behind her. Manon thought back to the vague reasons her parents had given whenever she'd asked why they'd left France to live in San Francisco. "Because of your father's work," Camille had always explained. And every time Manon had tried to ask if her mother had found it hard to leave her family and friends, she had replied with a smile and a shrug. But, Manon realized now, her mother had always said "because of," never "thanks to." The detective was right—a person didn't move to the other side of the globe over a simple fling. Manon felt angry with herself for not figuring this out sooner. Then she felt angry with her mother for never telling her. She would have loved to have been confided in, to hear her mother tell the story of a passionate love affair—especially one she'd personally experienced. Who was this man who'd stolen her heart? What must he have looked like? What had he promised her to sweep her off her feet? Had they only exchanged words and stolen moments, or had they loved each other with every part of themselves?

"And you think Thomas knew about all this?" she asked.

"Only you can answer that question—you know him better than I do. I've never even met the man. You still don't think he's guilty, do you?" Pilguez asked on his way to the door.

"I don't know," Manon replied. "Maybe he was clumsy by the altar, but the rest . . . no, no. It's impossible."

"I have a hard time believing it too. That said, I doubt his presence at the Columbarium was a simple coincidence."

Manon remained silent for a moment. "Maybe he was hoping to bring his father's remains there someday?"

"Maybe, maybe not. Did he tell you where he was staying?"

"No, but you'd be too late, anyway," Manon told him. "He's already gone. His plane left this afternoon."

"Here's hoping that urn magically reappears so I can close this case and save myself a ton of paperwork. If you see him again, ask him about it. You never know."

Pilguez said goodbye and walked out of the bookstore, pointing menacingly at her car as he left, to remind her about their agreement.

Thomas hadn't said a word in quite some time. Every now and again he stood up and paced the room, glancing at his suitcase and then at his father, before returning to the couch, a gloomy look on his face. Finally, Raymond couldn't stand it anymore.

"What on earth is bothering you?"

"The idea of leaving you alone on our last night together. The idea that it's our last night together at all."

"I saw there's a match at Levi's Stadium this afternoon. American football, but still—it would bring back some good memories. I don't know if you remember—you must have been about eight, I think—but you used to love the Paris Saint-Germain soccer team. One day, after they'd lost their third game in a row, I threw my newspaper to the ground and told you that I was done with them for good, just to tease you. I swore to cheer for their archrivals, the Olympique de Marseille, from that day on. You wouldn't talk to me for over a week. I thought it was hysterical, right up until your mother asked me to put a stop to it, explaining that you were truly upset. I went to see you in your room that night to apologize and explain, but you were hard to convince."

"I don't really feel like going to a game," Thomas said quietly.

"Do you know what you said to me that night? That I shouldn't give up when things get tough. You told me that I could cheer for whomever I wanted once PSG had won the title, but until then, they needed our support."

"So? I was eight."

"So, don't give up."

"On you?"

"No, on your passion for life. I need to know it's there, now more than I ever have before, or I'll feel guilty for eternity."

"Do you really want to go to the game?"

"What I would have really loved to do is take you out for ice cream. But that's beyond my means."

"How long?" Thomas said, looking directly at his father.

"You say that like I have a terminal illness."

The joke didn't even coax a smile from Thomas, who headed back toward the bedroom.

"I'm sorry." Raymond flickered and then reappeared in front of his son.

"I asked you how much time we have left."

"A few hours, maybe a day at most. I can tell they're calling me back. It's getting harder and harder for me to move around, and my vision is starting to get blurry up close. My hearing is going too. I must be getting old!"

"It looks to me like you're getting younger. And could you please stop with the dark humor? You're the only one who finds it funny."

"There's nothing funny to me about leaving you. But I've always found humor to be the most elegant strategy for dealing with adversity."

"What about compassion?"

"Compassion is a noble choice, son. Feel as much of it as you'd like. Just make sure you feel some for other people too."

Raymond sat down in front of the dark television screen. Thomas walked over to the coffee table, but before he could do anything, Raymond said, "Leave the remote alone. If I wanted to turn the TV on, I'd have done it myself."

"What do you want to do, then?"

"I want you to take me to see the Golden Gate Bridge, and to bring my urn."

"I'm happy to go there with you, but your ashes can stay here. You're not allowed to give up. I still need you."

Raymond nodded as his lips formed a crooked smile.

"Then call your friend Uber, and we'll have ourselves a day to remember!"

Manon was pacing, phone in hand. She had just chased out a customer, claiming she had to close early to do inventory. Ever since the detective had left, she'd been tormented by conflicting thoughts. She nearly canceled the dinner plans ten different times, but she kept changing her mind for reasons that eluded her. The heat was stifling, so she turned on the air conditioning before returning to her desk.

As she worked, she couldn't seem to add properly, and she even had to void one purchase order and start over. She also spent a long time searching for her accounting ledger, which she finally located on the international literature table. As she picked it up, the breeze from the air conditioner's fan suddenly reminded her of a merry-go-round long buried under the sands of time. The wooden horses started spinning, taking her back to forgotten summers.

A little girl clutching a golden mane. Her mother sitting on a bench, looking on. And next to her, a man who waved his hat and smiled, a little boy driving a fire truck by his feet.

The car wound down El Camino del Mar on its way to the ocean. Raymond wanted the driver to stop for a minute in front of a property located at the top of Sea Cliff Avenue. He pressed his head against the car's window and studied its facade.

"What did you do after my death?" he asked distractedly.

"I played concert after concert."

"Just as I hoped."

"What do you mean?"

"I hoped you wouldn't fall into despair. That you wouldn't blame the world for your misery. Really, I just didn't want you to be sad. Well, a little sad, but only the minimal amount of sadness, if you know what I mean."

"Not really."

"And after that? You couldn't have spent all your time in concert halls."

"Well, there was Sophie."

"Ah, Sophie. And then?"

"I haven't been with as many women as you might imagine."

"I'm asking what you did with your *life.*"

"I'm a pianist. I play the piano! What else should I be doing?"

"I'm going to share a little secret with you—and not just any secret. I was a surgeon, and I spent my life operating."

"That's hardly a secret."

"You're so impatient! The secret is that spending my life working was incredibly stupid. All those days and nights I stayed at the hospital instead of going for a walk with you or laughing with your mother."

"Are you telling me to give up my career so I can go for more walks?"

"You can be so annoying, Thomas. I'm just saying that someday, when you're happy, I hope you do everything you can to stay that way. Just think of all the things I missed. Think of the time we should have spent together."

"It's a little late for this now, don't you think?"

"If you have something to say, say it. Now's the time. I'm sure you'll feel lighter afterward."

Thomas kicked a can on the side of the road and sent it flying.

"You left without saying goodbye. I wasn't ready."

"That's why I came back."

"You came back for Camille."

"I didn't have time to say goodbye. You were traveling the world, and I was always waiting for you to come home. I didn't know my heart was going to stop beating one morning. I wouldn't make the same mistake again, I promise."

"Why are we stopped in front of this house?" Thomas glanced toward the window.

"I came to say goodbye." His father sighed.

"This is where she lived?"

"Yes, and now it's her place of eternal rest," Raymond said. "He took her home with him. As if holding her hostage for more than twenty years wasn't enough! Let's go."

The car set off again, making its way down a small road to the parking lot near Baker Beach. Thomas asked the driver to wait, saying he needed to get some fresh air before returning to the city.

"I figured as much," the driver replied with a chuckle. "Got any extra?" he asked with a wink. "I'll give you the ride and the wait for free."

"What are you talking about?" Thomas asked, surprised.

"You and your imaginary friend have been chatting away for the last twenty minutes. It must be some good stuff you're on. Sometimes I feel lonely at night in my car. I wouldn't mind a sample of whatever it is you're smoking."

"I'd rather pay for the ride," Thomas replied as he opened the door. "And you probably shouldn't smoke while you're driving."

Raymond walked over to the ocean, then turned around, his eyes glued to the house they'd stopped in front of earlier. Its white paintwork and blue shutters stood out up on the hill.

"Baker Beach will be perfect," he said. "I'll go for walks now and then, and if I'm lucky, she'll see me from the window. It's not what I imagined for the two of us, but it's not always possible to get what we want. And I have to admit, the view is incredible."

"Maybe for you," Thomas grumbled.

"Don't be selfish. You have your whole life ahead of you. You get to decide what to do with it. But whenever you play at Davies Symphony Hall—and I know you will—come for a walk on this beach. Here, more than anywhere else, you'll think of me with joy."

"That picture doesn't seem so joyful to me."

"Because you're seeing the glass as half empty. You're thinking of my absence instead of thinking about what we've had. Think instead about everything we've done together. Do you remember our bicycle tour, when I took you to see the châteaux of the Loire Valley? I made you pedal all day long, and then in the evenings—"

"You took me to see the music and light shows at the châteaux—Chambord, Cheverny, Blois, Chaumont. I was so sore I could hardly sit."

"Don't forget Amboise! We stayed up so late. We both felt exhausted and awestruck, all at once. One day you'll take that trip with your son or daughter, and you'll look back at them the whole time you're pedaling. Maybe that's what it means to be a father—you lead the way, but you also keep looking back to check on your children."

Thomas took a few steps forward, sat down on the sand, and studied the horizon. His father joined him, then nudged him in the side, his elbow passing through his son's jacket.

"We're going to be late for your dinner. Speaking of which, can I come along?"

"How could I possibly say no?"

"I promise to be discreet. I'll keep my distance. I'll sit at the bar and eavesdrop on my neighbors. Maybe it will help me remember some of my English. I could use a refresher. Who knows who I'll run into when I get there?"

"What is it like there?"

"Let's get going. You should never make a woman wait."

As they walked back to the car, Raymond stopped short and gave Thomas a funny little smile. "Pick up some of this dried seaweed, put it in your pocket, and give it to the driver. Then promise him that he'll have an unforgettable evening."

The sun had set over the city, and Manon still hadn't filled up a single page of her inventory log. Her thoughts were elsewhere, far from the bookstore and from San Francisco.

The wooden horses had turned into ponies, walking in circles through the sand of an arena, held by their reins.

Camille would wave distractedly whenever Manon passed by, and the man who sat on the bench talking to her was holding her hand, paying no attention at all to his little boy, who trotted proudly by.

There was a knock on the window, and Manon jumped when she saw Thomas waving at her.

"I hope I'm not too late," he said as he opened the door.

"I completely lost track of time."

"We're still on for dinner, right?"

As she went to get her raincoat, Thomas called after her that the sky was clear. She looked out the window and saw he was right, but still grabbed an umbrella before locking up.

"That's it?" Thomas asked.

"What do you mean?"

"No alarm? No security gate? Is the city really that safe?"

"No, of course not. I have both," she said, heading back to the store.

When the gate was halfway down, Thomas suggested she pause a minute.

"What now?" Manon asked worriedly.

"I just have one last question. Do you happen to sell purses?"

"What a strange question. It's a bookstore."

"That's what I thought. So, maybe the one I see in the window is yours?"

Manon opened the door, grabbed her bag, and set the alarm.

"Are you okay?" Thomas asked as they made their way toward the square.

"Since you arrived? Yes, just great. I made us a reservation . . . at which restaurant again? Oh yes, a table for two at Greens. It's behind the Fort Mason Center for Arts and Culture, on the wharf. The food is vegetarian; I hope you don't mind. I eat dairy, eggs, and fish, but I stopped eating meat. Animals are already obsessed with eating each other. If we do it, too, soon there won't be any left."

"I don't think cows and sheep are carnivores," Thomas replied, watching her carefully.

"True, but you get what I mean."

"Are you sure you're okay?"

"Wait a second. I have a car. Normally, I park it in front of the store and . . ."

They had already walked at least a hundred yards when she turned around.

"It's still there. I haven't said a word, so he has no reason to do anything."

"Has someone threatened you?"

"Not exactly . . . It has to do with a contract of sorts. The details would bore you to death."

Thomas picked up his pace to keep up with Manon, who was taking large strides.

"Do you want me to drive?"

She wasn't listening. She was preoccupied with looking for her keys in her bag. When she finally found them, she opened the passenger door and gestured for Thomas to get in.

"Do you think it's inappropriate?" she asked as they made their way toward the water.

"Running two red lights in a row? Not at all. It happens to the best of us."

"Having dinner with a stranger the night after my mother's funeral. I mean, you're not a *total* stranger, so I guess it's okay."

"Did you have a bad day?"

"A surprising one."

"Good surprising or bad?"

"I'm not sure . . . And I didn't get a thing done all afternoon. So, yes, I guess you could say I had a pretty bad day."

"Focus on the road and we'll talk about it at dinner."

Manon abruptly pulled off the road and parked in front of an old garrison.

"It used to be a fort," she explained as she got out of the car. "Now these buildings are home to a museum, a theater, and an organic market. And our restaurant."

Thomas opened the door to the restaurant and let Manon go in first. Once inside, he noticed his father sitting at the bar, winking at him. Startled, he didn't even notice as the hostess greeted them.

"Would you rather have dinner with her?" Manon asked.

"Who?" Thomas asked, caught off guard.

"The woman at the bar. She doesn't seem to mind you staring at her."

Thomas headed toward their table without answering. The waiter handed them two menus, which they studied in total silence. Thomas didn't understand a single thing written there. "Do you know what 'chickpea hush puppies' might involve? Or an 'urban macro bowl'?"

Manon ordered an avocado salad with spicy tofu and Thomas followed her lead.

"When my dad died," he said, "I told myself I wasn't allowed to cry, not even at the funeral. Then, a few days later, I just fell apart. I understand if your mind is elsewhere. Don't feel obligated to stay if you don't feel like it."

"You're so full of contradictions," Manon remarked.

"How do you mean?"

"On the one hand, you're a perfect gentleman, and on the other, you're utterly shameless."

Thomas frowned. "Did I say something to upset you?"

"Mom always made me wear a riding helmet before getting on a pony. I felt ridiculous, because all the other kids were allowed to ride without one. A little boy in my group used to mock me, calling me 'coconut.' Later, that same boy gave me his crepe when my mom had forgotten her wallet. Another time, he jumped onto the sandcastle I had spent the whole afternoon building, but then the next day, he helped me build a new one. One day, while I was eating ice cream, he elbowed me, and the cone smooshed into my face, making everybody laugh—even my mother laughed at me. Then that little monster helped me up when I fell off the swings and ran to get my mom so she could take care of my knee. And while she bandaged it, he sat there and consoled me. Now, Thomas, are you going to tell me what you were doing at her funeral, and why you lied to me?"

Thomas looked straight into her eyes.

"Another summer," he replied, "the little girl stole my blue truck and broke it on purpose. It was a gift from my father, and I really loved it. As for me, my dad always made me wear a hat in the sun, even though the other kids on the beach never did. He bought me a sailor's cap with a yellow anchor on the brim—a source of endless humiliation. A terrible little girl, whom I nevertheless dreamed of being friends with, always made fun of it, calling me Popeye. I recognized you immediately, as soon as I saw you in the mausoleum."

"Good for you, but you haven't answered my question."

"I came because my father wanted to attend the ceremony."

"But your father's dead, so . . ." Manon downed her glass of wine in one go. "Did he tell you that in his will?"

"No, he told me himself."

"Your father told you that when my mother died, he wanted you to go to the funeral?"

"Not exactly. He wanted to be there himself."

"But he's dead . . ."

"Yes, has been for five years."

Manon waved the waiter over to bring her a second drink.

"I'm sorry, but something isn't clicking for me."

"If I tell you my story, you'll think I'm crazy, which would be a shame, since you're probably the only person in the world I could ever share it with."

Manon guzzled her second glass and placed it back on the table. She then wiped her lips with the back of her hand like a pirate and looked right into Thomas's eyes, daring him to continue.

Thomas held her gaze and told how it all had started—the story of a strange cigarette and a ghostly apparition.

"I realize it's hard to accept," he said. "I had a terrible time believing it myself."

"So, your father came back from the afterworld to ask you to take him to my mother's funeral?" Manon said as the waiter filled her glass again.

"I get the sense that the afterworld is quite different from what we imagine. I've tried to drag more out of him several times, but he refuses to say any more. He says if he spills the beans, they'll call him right back."

"They . . . ," she said, then clicked her tongue.

"Yes, well, I'm afraid that's as much as I know. But if it makes you feel any better, Dad didn't come back in a shroud, or dragging a ball and chain behind him," Thomas said, with an uneasy laugh.

"So, how *did* he appear?" Manon asked pointedly. "I'm simply curious, of course."

"Like I said, in the armchair he used to read in. The first time, anyway."

"Yes, but how did he *look*?" Manon pressed.

"Ah, I see. Like he always did. White button-down shirt, tweed pants, tailored jacket. But a little younger than when he died."

Manon nodded, pursed her lips, and took a big sip of wine.

"And he flew on the plane with you?"

"Yes, and thank goodness he did. A passenger passed out during the flight and we saved him. Or, rather, Dad did. I just followed his instructions."

"And why wouldn't you? You're not a doctor, after all." Manon's words were thick with sarcasm that Thomas failed to notice.

"That's what the lady next to me kept pointing out, but no one listened to her. She worked herself into quite a state. I thought it was rather funny."

"I bet. And then what? Did you land the plane too?"

"No, but what happened next is even more unlikely. I hardly know where to begin."

"Stop! I've heard enough. With an imagination like that, you should give up the piano and become a writer. Really, you'd be a huge success. And that's coming from a bookseller. That said, I hope you won't mind if I'm not among your future readers. Fantasy isn't my cup of tea."

"You don't believe a single word I've said, do you?"

"Consider it from my point of view. What would you say if you were me?"

"I would quote a book I read a long time ago."

"And what would this book of yours say?"

"That even stories that seem impossible can become real if just two people believe in them. Can I ask you a question now?"

"You might as well . . ."

"Back when we were kids and our parents loved each other from afar, did you listen to bedtime stories about fairies and demons? Did you believe in those creatures and their incredible powers? Did you dream about fantastic worlds?"

"Of course I did. Just like all kids do."

"So, what's changed since then?"

"The woman who read me those stories left me. Yesterday, in fact," Manon replied.

"Well, my father came back to tell me one more story, and it reminded me why I became a pianist in the first place. So, I did my best to believe him, even if it made me look crazy. Now it's my turn to ask you to put yourself in my shoes. Imagine that one morning or evening, tomorrow or five years from now, your mother appears before you and asks you for a favor. A favor that will determine what the rest of eternity will be like for her. What will you do? Will you risk looking like a crazy person, or will you turn your back on her?"

As Manon signaled for another glass, Thomas remarked that this would be her fourth.

"I was hoping to take my mind off my mom tonight, but the guy I asked to dinner keeps telling me about his travels with his dad's ghost. Given the circumstances, I don't think drinking a bottle of Bordeaux is my biggest problem," she replied, a little tipsy despite her assurances.

Thomas glanced briefly toward the bar, where Raymond seemed to be having a grand time eavesdropping on a young couple's conversation.

Manon noticed. "I can't believe I made a scene about you looking at that woman when we came in. It was your dad all along, wasn't it?"

Thomas was quiet for a moment. "I'll ask for the check and take you home," he offered.

"No way. The night is young, and I'd kill for some dessert."

Manon snapped her fingers to call over the waiter. "I need a little something. Whatever you have, as long as it's chocolate. With two spoons, please. And another glass of wine," she called after him. Then she turned to Thomas. "Do you like chocolate?"

"Yes. You're right, I was looking at him. I said he could come if he promised to keep at a fair distance."

"Your conviction is quite appealing." Manon sighed.

"I thought it was my awkwardness you found charming."

"My mother and your father. Have you known for a long time?"

"No, he told me when he came back, and only because he needed my help."

"Otherwise he would have taken the secret to his grave, obviously," she replied in an ironic tone. "Tell me everything. After all, it's as much my business as yours."

"There's not a lot I can tell you, beyond the fact that they loved each other for over twenty years, seeing each other only during the summers at first. Then, loving one another from afar once your parents moved here."

"That's your father's version, or maybe another of your fantasies! There's no proof that it was anything more than a little fling."

"This is why I decided to keep quiet when we saw each other. I never lied, though. How would you have reacted if I had introduced myself and shared all this right away?"

"I would have asked you to leave immediately, as you know perfectly well. That's why you didn't say anything."

"Exactly. I regret it, though."

"Why?"

"Finish your dessert and I'll take you home. You can't drive, and our parents' past would make anything else too complicated."

"What do you mean 'anything else'?"

"I'm sorry, he does whatever he wants." Thomas sighed, glancing at the neighboring table.

Manon followed his gaze and burst out laughing. "Is he sitting there now?"

Raymond gave Thomas a mischievous glance and reassured him that he would get him out of the hole he'd just dug his son into. Thomas found himself once again speaking words that weren't his own.

"It was a gray afternoon. You and your mother were wearing matching blue flowered dresses; you looked like sisters. My father gave you some caramels, and your mother let you take them. The two of them were sitting on a bench, discreetly holding hands while you played hopscotch. You came up to them and asked who the man was. Your mother replied, 'A summer friend, sweetheart,' and you ran off to play again, carefree and happy. When fall came, you asked your mother about the man who'd given you the caramels. She knelt down and told you the truth this time—that he was very dear to her. She made you promise to keep the secret.

"The year you turned ten, you were practically a shoo-in to win a dance competition, but then you broke your collarbone when you slipped on a balance beam during a gymnastics class. You were inconsolable, and your mother took you to New Mexico to take your mind off things. Your mother-daughter trip became a ritual, and every year after that, at Thanksgiving, you traveled together: Antelope Canyon in Arizona, Great Salt Lake in Utah, Yellowstone, New Orleans, Niagara Falls, Baton Rouge and the Mississippi River, Mount Rushmore. Then, for your sixteenth birthday, she took you to Rome and Venice.

"You were a good student, but you had a tendency to talk back, which nearly got you thrown out of Lowell High. Your father made a donation, and the school agreed to look the other way. At fifteen, you loved ice hockey and you cheered for the San José Sharks. Your mother suspected you had a crush on Bill Lindsay."

"That's ridiculous. Bill Lindsay was hideous. I was in love with Todd Harvey, and I was *seventeen*! And how do you know all that?"

The waiter brought the bill in a leather check holder and placed it down in front of Thomas.

"I'll get it. That was the agreement," Manon said as she tried to grab it.

But Thomas had already discreetly handed his card to the waiter earlier. He signed the receipt and put his wallet away.

"I don't know how you managed that little card trick," she protested. "I didn't see a thing."

"My awkwardness is a great distraction," Thomas replied as he stood up.

He stopped at the neighboring table and asked his father to make his own way home. Raymond sighed and disappeared.

Manon staggered through the parking lot. When they got to the car, she threw her keys to Thomas and told him her address.

Silence hung over them for a long time after they left Fort Mason. Finally, as the Prius made its way up California Street, she broke the spell.

"Why not, I guess," she said. "Everyone experiences grief differently. If you still need your father to exist, then who am I to stand in your way? Besides, I'm not much of a drinker, but I'm quite drunk now. I'm sure I'll wake up with a monumental migraine in the morning—I can already feel one coming on—and none of this will have ever happened."

"That's what I told myself, too, after the joint."

"Right. So, how did you know all those things about me?"

They had just arrived in front of her building, and Thomas parked the car along the sidewalk. He turned around to grab the bag he'd left on the back seat and placed it on Manon's lap.

"Here, you should have these."

"What's this?"

"A box of letters from your mother that my father kept. If you ever find the ones he wrote to her, I'd really love to have them. I wrote to you too—an email explaining everything, but I didn't send it. I was too afraid you'd never want to talk to me again. I copied it down on paper instead and left it at the bottom of the bag."

Manon stared at Thomas, unable to speak a single word, incapable of understanding the emotions that arose in her as she prepared to say goodbye. She wanted to stay and hear him talk more about her childhood, and share more about her mother. She wanted to ask him a thousand questions, without any attitude or skepticism this time, even if there was nothing logical about any of this, just to hear his voice. She didn't want to go home alone. But Thomas was quiet, so she got out of the Prius. After a moment, she came back.

"I just remembered, this is my car."

"Of course." Thomas apologized and returned her keys. "I'll walk you to your door."

"I can make it on my own," she insisted as she made her way toward the building.

"I'm not so sure," Thomas replied. He reached her just as she slid down the railing she was leaning against. He helped her up, waited for her vertigo to dissipate, and then supported her as she climbed the stoop.

They walked up the stairs to the next floor together, and Thomas waited for her to open her door.

"Do you think you can make it to your bed?"

"It's a studio. I think I'll be okay. Wait, don't leave yet. What did you mean when you said that our parents' past would make 'anything else' too complicated?"

Thomas looked straight at her, then drew close to her and kissed her quickly.

"Good night, Manon."

19

After going inside, Manon took a long shower that sobered her up, but didn't soothe her migraine. It was already three o'clock in the morning on Friday.

She put on an oversize T-shirt and sat cross-legged on the rug. She stared at the box of letters for a while before finding the courage to open it. At last, she took a deep breath and lifted the lid.

Emotion overwhelmed her when she saw all the envelopes in her mother's handwriting. She picked up the first letter addressed to Raymond.

> My distant but dearest love,
> It's been a year. The apartment we moved into isn't very big. I miss my house in France so much, though not as much as I miss you, and yet the memories feel linked. I've made my bedroom my refuge and filled it with the souvenirs I have left: a few photos you took one summer. I admire them as one admires a sunset, equal parts wonder and sadness to see the day end, mixed with hope that the morning will come soon.
>
> I put my cherry bookcase in the small entryway. It holds all the books I love, books I've spent so many evenings with. All the stories we liked to talk about on that bench. The living room is big and bright, and

the windows look out over the bay. The timeworn furniture reflects the sunlight. I covered the couch in a colorful blanket. Do you remember it? The one you admired in the shop on La Grande Rue? The next day, I went back to buy it in secret. Sitting at my desk to write to you, I can take in the entire San Francisco Bay. The Bay Bridge and Telegraph Hill crowned with Coit Tower—such a strange name, don't you think?—are to my right. An unusual woman had it built after her death, if you can imagine. She smoked cigars and wore long pants before it was socially acceptable. She was an incorrigible gambler and dressed like a man to get into the casinos that didn't allow the fairer sex. An admirable woman whose courage I would love to possess. She left her fortune to the city. For years, men watched for incoming ships from the top of the tower. I've gone up there and watched the horizon myself. I realize nothing I'm telling you is particularly interesting, but what can I say without hurting you? Manon is getting used to her new life. I was so afraid our hurried departure would upset her. She's already speaking English, or at least she manages quite well. She's my confidante and my best friend, so much so that I sometimes forget to be the loving mother she needs. She's grown so much. I already catch glimpses of the remarkable young woman she will become someday. She's headstrong, which I try to temper as best I can, while hiding the wonder she inspires in me each day. She started dance when we got here, and her teacher tells me she's particularly gifted. I hope she won't want to become a ballerina, though. It's a profession full of suffering. But if she wants to, I won't stand in her way. Nothing can really resist her strong will and rebellious spirit.

It's three o'clock in the afternoon—almost time to pick her up from school. The weather is lovely today. My windows are open and I can hear the cable cars clicking as they travel the city. You're allowed to ride them standing on the outside steps. The wind lifts your hair and the feeling is intoxicating, a little like riding an old Parisian bus in the times when you could stand on the back platform.

In the evening, the smell of the tide wafts up from the ocean and carries me far away from here. I breathe in the fragrance of another sea, the one where we watched side by side as the waves crashed over the peninsula or the fishing boats came back to port in the evening.

You are the one person to whom I feel I can say anything, the one person who loves and understands me. So, I know that you'll understand what my words aim to say, despite their clumsiness.

My love, you were my whole world. You must know that I never really left, since my memories of you are still here, like a song in my heart.

Camille

Manon folded up the letter and put it back in its envelope, then took out another.

My distant but dearest love,

I was so pleased to get your letter. I went to the post office, as I do every Thursday. Whenever I go, I feel like a spy collecting information of utmost importance. In fact, that's close to the truth, isn't it?

But no one ever follows me. Manon is at school, and he's always traveling.

I really don't want to worry you, but in order for you to understand what I'm about to write, I first have to tell you that I had a little fainting spell recently. Nothing serious, I promise. You're a doctor, and I would never lie to you. But when I passed out in the street, I thought I was dying. When I came to, I was terrified—not by how I felt, but by the idea that something might happen to me before I have a chance to say all that I must say to you.

When Manon goes to bed, the house is empty. You're not here, you who brought me back to life ten years ago. I was a mother and nothing more, fulfilled by my daughter alone. I lived for her, and my only goal was to make her happy. My days followed her rhythm. I took her to school in the morning, and then waited to pick her up in the afternoon. We would walk home, hand in hand, and then she'd sit next to me and draw until bedtime. When school was out and the weather was good, we had picnics in the backyard. During breaks, we would often sleep in the same bed, since her father was only ever home on the weekends.

It was noon on a gorgeous summer day. The ocean was calm, and there wasn't even the slightest breeze. Tiny waves petered out at our feet. The beach was deserted as Manon, sitting in an abandoned rowboat on the sand, tore into her sandwich.

I was reading when I heard a man's voice behind me. "If this little girl didn't have such a pretty mother, I would give her a serious talking to."

I looked up and met your gaze. "Why is that?" I said, nearly furious.

"Because I spent the morning cleaning my boat and now she's filling it with crumbs," you replied.

You left and came back a little later with a bottle of rosé and two glasses. Your son was taking riding lessons nearby, and you suggested I enroll my daughter. You were so handsome, so tall. Your eyes had just brought the woman in me—dead for quite some time—back to life. A person doesn't get to choose who they love.

I enrolled my daughter in riding lessons. Every day, we sat on a bench, watching our children, and you respected my silence. You were gracious enough to never tell me about your life, and I did the same. The moments we shared belonged only to the present and to us. One day, Manon came over to you and said, "I think Mom really likes you," and I blushed.

You know the rest, my love, but I had to tell you about the wonderful gift you've given me. Manon has become a young woman and, thanks to you, so have I. For eternity.

It's so hard to do the right thing.

Camille

Manon kept reading through the night, until she reached the last letter her mother had written. Then, just before going to bed, she remembered what Thomas had said. She hurried over to the bag and found the letter he'd left for her.

As the sun rose, she opened her window and breathed in the smell of the tide as it wafted up from the bay.

20

At ten o'clock on Friday morning, the car was making its way to Baker Beach. Sitting next to Thomas, Raymond lovingly placed his hand over his son's.

"We're lucky the weather's nice," he said.

Thomas stayed quiet.

"Did your evening end well?"

"Couldn't have gone better."

"Ah, and who gets the credit for that?" his father asked. "She certainly could drink, though. Then again, who could blame her? You chose an excellent vintage."

"You taught me how to choose a good wine."

"Really? I had forgotten."

"I'm going to miss you so much," Thomas mumbled.

"I know. I'll miss you too. But now it's my chance to watch over you. We each get a turn."

"Will you be happy there?"

"Don't worry, I know how to make myself content. I spent my whole life chasing little moments of happiness, and I even managed to enjoy a few, including the day you were born. I'll do just fine. How do you think I was able to arrange this leave in the first place? Do you know anyone more resourceful than your dad?"

"I certainly don't know anyone who has more pride. I got that from you too."

"Just be careful to keep it in check, son."

The car got as close as possible to the water, coming to a stop in the deserted Baker Beach parking lot. This time, Thomas told the driver not to wait.

He opened the door, grabbed his suitcase, and gestured to his father to follow.

They stepped onto the sand. Raymond looked around and pointed to a dune.

"Up there would be perfect," he said.

Thomas had begun climbing when his phone vibrated in his pocket.

"Where are you?" Manon asked.

"At Baker Beach," he answered.

"I'll be there in twenty minutes, tops."

"I think I should be alone."

"I know what you're about to do. I read your letter."

"Are you familiar with the crazy guy who wrote it?"

"I met a pianist once who promised me that any story, no matter how crazy, could become real if two people believed in it together. I want him to keep that promise. You were there for Mom; I want to be there for your father. Wait for me."

Raymond was taking in the view from the top of the dune. Thomas joined him and sat down.

"It's considered rude to make a lady wait, and yet we spend our whole lives waiting for them. It's unfair, but what can we do?"

"So, you listen to my phone calls now too?"

"It's not my fault. Sound waves work in mysterious ways. Speaking of which, it's strange, but I can hear music in my head."

"It might be the melody I composed last night."

"So, you're a composer now?"

"I always have been, I've just never let anyone listen."

"You're wrong to keep it to yourself. It's beautiful. It sounds like the refrain of a song. Have you given it a title?"

Thomas told him that he had. "'Ghost in Love.'"

Raymond looked at his son with the lopsided smile he always used to hide his feelings.

The two of them sat there, side by side, in total silence. Every now and then, Thomas would look at his watch, and his father would tell him not to worry. She was on her way. And the more time passed, the more Raymond perked up.

"There she is," he suddenly exclaimed. "Get up and welcome her. It's the least you can do. And dust off the bottom of your pants, they're covered in sand."

Manon was wearing black jeans and a tailored white top. She carried a big linen bag over her shoulder that added a touch of elegance to her delicate appearance.

She climbed up the dune and arrived breathless at the top.

"I drove as fast as I could," she said, placing her bag down next to Thomas's.

He watched her without a word, and she came forward and kissed him.

"You were right, I remember everything now. I read Mom's letters last night, and your letter, too, and . . ."

She looked at the bags at their feet, their handles already entangled.

"I don't really know how to accomplish their last wishes," she said.

Thomas leaned over and took out his father's urn. Manon did the same with her mother's.

"I went to get her for this last trip. Dad was adamantly against it, but I didn't really give him a choice. We fought and he'll be mad at me for weeks, but he'll get over it. He's never been able to hold a grudge for long when it comes to me. Do we need to say anything in particular?" she asked worriedly.

Raymond gestured to Thomas that there was no need. Time was running out. But this time, Thomas was the one who did as he pleased.

"No one should be asked to bury their parents twice—not even by their parents. So, we're going to do things differently this time."

"Is he here?" Manon asked.

Thomas nodded. Raymond was watching them, his impatience palpable.

"And Mom, do you see her?"

"No, but he says she's here too. Let's open the urns. He can barely hold still."

They took out the vessels carefully. Thomas poured his father's ashes into Camille's urn and announced, "By the powers you vested in us, we declare you united for all eternity."

Manon looked at him for a long moment, seemingly close to laughter.

"You forgot to say they could kiss. That usually comes next," she said.

Then Thomas gave the urn a good shake, just like his father had asked him to do.

As Manon scattered their ashes, Camille's silhouette appeared on the beach. She was radiant as she took her summer companion passionately in her arms.

"Well, I think we're all set for the kiss," Thomas announced.

Camille and Raymond turned toward their children. They both seemed so happy that Thomas couldn't help but smile. But Manon was watching only her pianist.

The two silhouettes began to fade slowly. Just before disappearing, Raymond asked Camille to excuse him for a moment so he could share a final word with his son.

He walked over to Thomas and whispered in his ear, "There is one thing I never said enough. It's the heart of everything, though, and the obvious answer to your question. I can't believe it took me so long to figure it out. Masculine bravado can go to hell, because heaven is the place where you say, I love you, son. That's what it means to be a father, and I will always be yours. For all eternity."

Epilogue

Three planes and one day later, Thomas made his way onto the stage at Warsaw's opera house, then sat down at his bench.

That night, he was playing Rachmaninoff again, but this time the Concerto No. 2 took him far beyond the Russian steppe, to the other side of the world, to Baker Beach in California.

When he began the second movement, he missed a note, scandalizing the conductor.

Thomas hadn't been able to resist the urge to scan the room.

Manon was sitting in the third row.

About the Author

Photo © 2023 David Ken

Marc Levy is the international bestselling author of twenty-six novels, including *A Woman Like Her*, *P.S. from Paris*, *All Those Things We Never Said*, *The Last of the Stanfields*, *The Strange Journey of Alice Pendelbury*, and *Just Like Heaven*, which was adapted into a hit film starring Reese Witherspoon. Marc's novels have been translated into fifty languages and have appeared on bestseller lists in several countries, including Sweden, Germany, Italy, Spain, Russia, and China. Their combined sales have surpassed fifty million worldwide. He is the most read contemporary French author in the world. For more information, visit www.marclevy.com.

About the Translator

Maren Baudet-Lackner is an American literary translator from the French who is passionate about bringing exceptional works of literature by underrepresented authors to English-speaking readers. She has published a dozen titles with major imprints in the United Kingdom and the United States and is the recipient of a 2023 PEN Presents award and 2023 Albertine Translation grant. Maren holds advanced degrees from Yale University and the Sorbonne and lives near Paris with her family. For more information, visit www.marenbaudet-lackner.com.